EUSTON,
we have a problem

Adam Kaczinsky

ADAM KACZINSKY

ISBN: 9781790419005

Imprint: Independently published

Cover photograph: Vlad Orlov/Adobe Stock

Copyright © 2018 Adam Kaczinsky

All rights reserved. No part of this publication may be reproduced, stored in a retrieval system, or transmitted, in any form or by any means, electronic, mechanical, photocopying, recording or otherwise, without the previous written permission of the Author.

EUSTON, WE HAVE A PROBLEM

En Saturno
Viven los hijos que nunca tuvimos

En Plutón
Aún se oyen gritos de amor

(On Saturn
Live the children we never had

On Pluto
You can still hear cries of love)

Pablo Alboran, "Saturno", 2017

ADAM KACZINSKY

EUSTON, WE HAVE A PROBLEM

I hope someday

We'll sit down together

And laugh with each other

About these days, these days

Rudimental, "These days", 2018

ADAM KACZINSKY

CONTENTS

1	Come on Barbie, let's go party	Pg 9
2	Matthias	Pg 18
3	Without Matthias	Pg 29
4	Pawel	Pg 36
5	Hot liquid	Pg 45
6	Olek	Pg 47
7	Dirty feelings	Pg 53
8	Chems	Pg 58
9	Gonorrhea	Pg 64
10	Fucking here and there	Pg 68
11	How it all started	Pg 85
12	Diego	Pg 94
13	Conservative environment	Pg 104
14	After the party	Pg 115
	Some statistics	Pg 120

ADAM KACZINSKY

1. COME ON BARBIE, LET'S GO PARTY

It's Saturday night and we're here at my place, living our lives to the fullest. I'm so excited to look at so many naked good-looking men in my flat, everyone having pleasure, no strings attached.

The atmosphere has gotten quiet now, Frank is getting sucked by a twink in the kitchen, three other blokes also doing some soft stuff while watching "X-factor" on the sofa. Davide's in the shower, I'm not sure if he's alone or not, and I'm lying on my bed while charging my phone and enjoying the view, feeling proud as a peacock.

For the last hour and a half, there has been some good action going on. Frank was sitting there on the couch, where the three blokes are now watching "X-factor" and Davide, a young slutty Italian bottom, was lying on him, Frank's hard big cock deep inside. Both legs up, open, each one touching one armrest, two guys licking Davide's feet. A third bloke behind the sofa, fulfilling his mouth. And me standing in front of the couch, double-penetrating him together with Frank. It was not only the heat I was feeling, rubbing my cock with Frank's inside that bitch's hole. It was also his moaning, almost screaming of pleasure, at the same time he was tightening a silver necklace between his teeth after his mouth got free.

The party started some 27 hours ago and now we're in the calm before the storm. The hype will be in a few hours when the hottest guys will finish their nights in clubs around and will pop by.

The first one to join the party on Friday was Frank. He's always the first one to arrive. Frank is a dealer, our exclusive provider of crystal meth, meph, and GHB. Not only does he have some really good stuff, but also I'd never have guessed this could be his job. In all these Netflix series, dealers never try the shit they sell, but Frank, he is enjoying it with us, he is having fun at the party. From time to time he leaves the place to sell something around, but he's always back with us as soon as he can. And he's muscled, hairy, with a huge cock, and always so participative, so I want him here.

Since I'm the host, I don't pay for any of the stuff. I think this deal is fair. I'm offering my flat and a lot of paying customers. But Frank is one of us, and he is also fair with the other frequent guests: they pay much less of London's market price, and in exchange they get great stuff, as well as Frank's great cock.

I got to know Frank just a few months ago. Before I met him, I was struggling, looking for chems on Grindr, always paying different prices and sometimes getting doubtful quality products. There was also a BYOB policy, you could take your own chems from home, but we've always been missing some of the chems.

Frank is living in the outskirts, sharing a flat, and I'm sure from the day he started working at my place on weekends, he improved his profits by a lot.

EUSTON, WE HAVE A PROBLEM

When I started to host parties at home, I knew it would work out well. First of all, because of the position. Being centrally located just minutes away from Euston station, we are able to catch a wide public, from the local party bitches in Camden, to the horny straight bloke coming out of a concert at Koko or the guy from the outskirts just arriving or waiting for his train. And also people staying in Soho, which is just three stops away by tube.

It was a good deal when a few years ago I rented this small loft in Eversholt Street for 1250 pounds per month. At that time it was too expensive for me, but I really wanted to be centrally located, no need to pass half of my day traveling to the office and back, or not having the opportunity to go out for a dinner in the center. Now I can say it was a bargain.

Under my loft, in the basement, there's only a Chinese massage workshop, so nobody is complaining if a lot of people are going in and out at any time during the weekend. They're also open 24 hours, but we can make some noise. Up to today, nobody ever complained. Who knows, maybe also because they may be illegal workers and don't want to look for problems.

The flat is small, but it is all one space, so I can always keep control of everything and everyone. When I started the chemsex parties, my bed wasn't big enough for so many visitors, so I've found the necessary space to put a sofa. I've bought a faux leather skin one, which is easy and fast to clean.

My guests love my parties because here they can feel like they're at home. First of all, it is the cheapest option to pass a full weekend. You don't have to pay the entrance to a club, don't have to pay for expensive drinks. And most important of all, sex is guaranteed.

The only expense is for the chems, but you can always bring your own stuff from home. What I didn't like at some chems parties I've been to, was the sense of not being safe. It never happened to me, but many of the people I met have been robbed by people that were coming only for a while and took advantage of them being on drugs, taking away all their valuables. When I was going there, whatever the action, I would always keep my socks on, and put all my money under the planters. I preferred to look like a shabby German tourist instead of being robbed. My mobile phone, well, always in my hands, connected to Grindr or watching some porn while having live fun.

When I realised my parties would work, I've found some cheap lockers at IKEA, like the ones at my office, and I bought a few of them. They are meant for the frequent visitors, and for the people that are supposed to stay for the whole weekend. They can easily put their belongings in the locker, and keep the keys always with them since the keys are attached to rubber bracelets. My guests love it, it is one problem less to be bothered about.

I have to admit that I am creative. My parties have an added value and visitors are feeling safer than anywhere else.

The atmosphere at a chemsex is relaxed, not judging. Someone is coming on Friday afternoon, staying till Sunday evening. Others are just joining us for a few hours after clubbing, jerking off and leaving. Last weekend we were 37, as far as I counted. At my place, every Friday is Black Friday, and you can get whatever you want at no cost.

It is a place where you can really feel free. Nobody is forcing you to do anything. If you don't do drugs, you can join as long as you're hot. We mostly don't use condoms. But if you want latex, feel free to use it. Most of us are on PrEP, so we have no risk if we fuck raw. And it is much more pleasant.

But this is also a place for socializing. The ones that stay for the whole weekend are people that want to feel they're part of a group, of a community, and here they have it. A lot of people are doing things in common, where nobody is judging, like my family and villagers were doing throughout my childhood, my school friends later, or like my boss is still doing.

And there is also a human touch, tactility and the possibility of breaking social barriers. There's no social difference on Grindr, everyone's here: the baker, the politician, the student, the music star, the unemployed. And we all come together.

As I use to say, it is not a one-night stand, it is a three nights stand of anonymous sex. You enjoy life to the max, but on Monday you have no obligations towards these people, like in conventional relationships. If you have liked it, you're welcome to join again the following Friday.

I don't understand why there is an aggressive media campaign against chemsex. Newspapers state that the Grindr-organised orgies are the latest horror, they only write about overdoses happening and create panic about the potential risks of getting infected. Until now I've never seen one serious overdose. And we're on PrEP, fuck it, no infection can happen. Those who are positive, they're taking medication and cannot transmit the virus either.

Also on Grindr, we sometimes get messages from people writing about STDs. All paranoid people. I use to reply to them that they're psychopaths, and then I block them. I don't want fucked up people to complicate my life. Here, we're happy.

I can remember how sad my life used to be, being at home alone watching Big Brother, missing someone to talk to, wanting a hug I was never able to get. I was lonely and anxious, and now I'm not anymore. Although it is an orgy and someone thinks it's impersonal, I've found the intimacy I was missing.

I enjoy that presence of strangers and often only watch. I had a friend in Poland who had a transplanted liver, couldn't drink any alcohol or even less smoke joints. He was working as a public relations guy for several clubs. He was able to stop tourists on the street, convince them to join his parties, where everyone would get free drinks or find marijuana to buy. Several times I joined him for a night out. It took me a while to remember his liver had been transplanted and he couldn't drink or smoke at all. And he didn't drink or smoke at all, all night long. He was convincing everyone to do it but had a big charisma that nobody was noticing that he was not doing anything. I feel a bit like him, but I'm not only watching. I'm also participating.

One time we had a guest that was only watching, not participating at all. He wrote us through Grindr, saying he was a journalist and was looking to participate in a chillout, that's how we call our parties, to understand how they worked. He would not take any drugs or participate in the action. It was an interesting proposition. Frank and I liked the idea, so we let him join the party. It would have been fun being observed, getting the attention of a journalist. I actually never asked him what media he was working for, but I wrote him he could join only if he was going to be naked. So he did. He was sitting naked for a few hours near the kitchen's table, while lots of action was going on around him. He had a notepad, and he was writing a few lines from time to time. The new people that were joining were not informed about who he was. But, actually, nobody cared.

EUSTON, WE HAVE A PROBLEM

Now in the kitchen, there's still the same twink on his knees, the one that was sucking Frank a few minutes ago. And with him, there's a big Greek hairy cub teaching him new Greek words with his cock. He shows his hard cock, saying "putsos", and then slapping the twink with his hand, saying "skampili". He's now slapping the boy with his cock, saying "putsos skampili". It seems that one of the three guys on the sofa is also greek because he's telling that *putsos* is a really vulgar word to say cock, and *skampili* is an archaic, almost stately word and that this is a big contrast. The two in the kitchen are not listening at all, and just continuing to enjoy their *putsos skampili* harder and harder.

Frank is dressing up, which probably means he's got to deliver something to a customer. On the couch there are four people now, one leaning on the armrest and being fucked hard, keeping the mobile phone in his hands and shouting: "Does anyone have an iPhone 5 charger? There's some bloke from Grindr that wants to join, and I'm getting out of battery". The other two are deeply concentrated on a song being sung by a participant in "X Factor".

To invite people to the party, I have a great list of contacts. I'm normally connected on Grindr Monday to Thursday, adding people to my potential guest list. Then during the weekend, wherever they are, I send bulk messages to any of them, and they're free to join.

Some may say we're not real friends. Well, maybe our friendship is not so deep, this is true. Most of them are saved in my contact list as "Chalk Farm power bottom", "XL Tottenham", "pig Mornington Crescent", "power top Baker st", "Arab Camden", "Regent Park sucker", "horny chub". But they're a good company, and we share a lot. We're a group with common interests, and I feel we pertain to a real community.

Another guy is just entering the flat. Crystal blue eyes, solid physique, such a handsome smile. He is putting his clothes off while the one fucking the guy on the couch is pulling him out, letting the new one have a turn.

When someone new is arriving, there's always this sense of euphoria, together with curiosity to see who it will be. What I know is that we're never too much.

What I really love at these parties is to fuck the ones that define themselves as only top, and get fucked by the ones that say they're bottom only. Call it a fetish, a challenge, but it's what makes me the most horny, together with the idea of having a wide option of potential partners wanting to fuck with me. Another fetish I have are huge cocks. If a cock is small, my arse just doesn't let it in. The only way to open myself is having in front of myself something really big.

I still remember my beginnings in London. Going out to Soho was a waste of money, and sex was not even guaranteed. Thanks to Grindr, all have become much cheaper and faster. Gay bars are now closing down, and we're here, in the comfort of my flat, enjoying life. I call myself a hedonist, an extreme one. We've got a life to enjoy it, and the chillouts are a way of life.

What I most hate about chemsex are Mondays, that's clear. Not only because I'm wasted. But also because I have to wait a full four and a half days to repeat.

Now there are six people together on the couch, going back and forth. Two of them leaning, the other four taking turns on the two bottoms. The action may look mechanical and boring, but I guarantee you here's the best fun in town. The crystal blue eyes bloke is having a solo a few meters away, waiting for a free ass, and someone is ringing the doorbell.

The hairy Greek cub is going to open, and there's a fucking good looking one entering. He's totally my type. I want him now. I have no clue who spoke to him, but I'm going to suck him right now.

His face sounds familiar. I know him from somewhere. Was he here last week? I don't think so.

Two months ago we were having a sweaty gangbang, the one bottom gay screaming of pleasure when a mate waiting in line to fuck him asked him if he was presenting the evening news at the BBC. And he did.

The new guy puts his clothes off and lies on my bed. I start to suck him passionately.

He's not presenting the news at the BBC, but I know him.

His cock in and out of my mouth, I cannot stop thinking about who he is.

Oh fuck, he was the last boyfriend of Matthias!

2. MATTHIAS

Matthias was my best friend, probably the only one I've ever had in London. But he's no longer alive. The man I'm now sucking may be one of the causes of this.

We knew each other from the very first week I arrived in London. Since I was new to the city and didn't know anyone here, I wrote a public announcement on CouchSurfing, looking to meet local people. He was the only one to reply.

We met on a Saturday afternoon in Shoreditch and had a walk to Brick Lane. There he took me to a great food hall with oriental street food, which became one of my favorite places to have lunch at weekends. We also went to a bar, called 1001, and sat on a table with a wooden bench in the courtyard, having a long chat. I'll not forget it, because we were sitting there for a while without ordering any drinks. On the way back home we passed through another bar he was claiming was the bar where Jack the Ripper was a frequent customer. On the way to it, in the narrow dark streets, he was telling me the stories of Jack the Ripper. Once in the bar, he asked me to go to the basement, where the toilets were situated. Since the toilets were so old, he claimed I peed in the same toilet as Jack the Ripper was in the past.

Almost all the places I know in London I saw for the first time with Matthias. He took me to Camden Town, and we passed a lot of afternoons lying together on the grass at Regent's Park. I was usually looking at the planes passing above us, wondering if they were taking off or landing, guessing if they were coming from Heathrow or the City and where they've been heading. I always loved airplanes. Inside them, there are hundreds of human life stories, hundreds of reasons why someone's in it. And they've always symbolized freedom for me. When I told him this, he replied that I was a real village boy. For city boys, airplanes are only a means of transportation.

Although he physically was not my type, we matched a lot. I was always feeling comfortable with him, and he was enjoying my presence too. My first Monday in London was a bank holiday, and he took me to the City. Still remember going up the elevator of the shopping center next to Saint Paul's Cathedral, getting the best perspective of the church, then passing the Millennium Bridge and seeing the Globe theater for the first time. One of my favorite spots now, the Sky Garden at the Walkie Talkie, I discovered with him. We were looking at the skyline of London at sunset when he told me that, on days when there's good visibility like today, if I look south I can even see Paris. And on the south side of The Thames, there was a small metal tower looking just like the Eiffel one.

We had roasted chicken at Nando's under the London Bridge so many times. It was one of the places he loved most. There he also had his favorite seat, on the first floor, facing the Thames and with stunning views. We didn't match only in one thing: I couldn't stand the lemon and herb *peri peri* sauce he was putting on his chicken.

But this was probably the only difference between us, the only thing we hadn't in common. He was a special person, a different kind of guy, very caring, and he slowly became my point of reference in a big city where one can get lost easily and feel deep loneliness.

I discovered the bad feeling of the big city after the first few months here. In the beginning, everything was new, I was meeting a lot of people. There was always a lot going on, an endless offer of museum expositions, musical shows and concerts. I loved the dark bricks on the walls of the building and the melancholic weather of the city.

But it took me not much time to discover the dark side of such a big place. Most of the day I was passing at my office in Canary Wharf, on the phone with customers, solving their problems. It was a big open space, and we were around six hundred people doing the same. But as in any multinational corporation, employers need to be productive, and our job is being on the phone. We barely had the opportunity to speak to each other during our short cigarette break downstairs. Our lunch break times were changing every day, so I never got to share even a lunch companion. For the company, everything that was mattering was our productivity per hour and the customers' satisfaction. For us that were working there, too, because a big part of our salary was based on these performance indicators.

This meant that I had around 600 hundred nice colleagues, but we've all been too busy to interact mutually. To comply with the standards of a big corporation, we were not behaving as humans.

After work, we were all wasted and everyone was running to their homes, someone was having children to take care of, others were having yoga classes, others were living far out of London and needed to catch a train. Everyone was already having a life, and the job was taking a great part of it.

I was coming back home and thinking about what to do before going back to the office the following morning. I'd love to have a nice dinner, I could afford it, or go to see a movie or theater play. I did this alone on some occasions, but I felt awkward. Then, I started to look for friends on Grindr.

When you're looking for friends on Grindr in a big city, you're searching for a needle in a haystack. It's not an easy job to find someone interested in something other than a fast hookup. Even the ones that were agreeing to come to see a movie or have a beer at my place would start to touch my cock two minutes after the movie would begin. I let them. If I had someone hugging me during the whole movie, to feel less alone, to feel human warmth, I could give part of my body for that feeling. But immediately after jerking off, they normally left, without seeing how the movie ended. They were going back to their boyfriends normally, or to another hookup. And I was not getting the hug and warm feeling I was looking for.

If the big city is superficial, the gay world is much more so. And I always thought the sense of loneliness in the whole community is very high, but for some reason, people are scared to create laces. In a big city, there are many opportunities, there's always someone that is better, sexier and more hung than the one we're staying with at this moment. And there's opportunities to meet him. So why give our full attention to someone if, there outside, there's much more than we can have?

But when you start to have more, you want to have even more. I didn't dislike hook-ups, although I was missing social interaction and human warmth. But with time I discovered people are really excited in Grindr while planning to meet, and very often absent while fucking. There's no eye contact. Many people I could read their minds, while they were fucking with me they were already thinking about their next sex date.

This is something happened to me with cigarettes. I was addicted, I needed a cigarette at any time and I was excited when I was lighting one, but at the moment I was smoking it, I was not enjoying it. I was thinking about the following one.

After work, alone in the city, I just needed a hug. But so many times I accepted to give my ass just to have some physical contact, not to feel isolated.

I was not proud of that, and when the sexual act was finished, I felt lonelier than before.

With time I somehow accepted that I'm meat that can be chosen from a catalog, and that I probably don't deserve and will not have anything better in life.

Matthias was a bright ray of light in this tunnel.

When we were together, we were complaining for hours about this superficial world.

He was telling me stories of people he was speaking to. He was not meeting people as often as me. He spoke to someone for about a month before even having coffee together. It was not easy for him to find people like him, but he knew what he was looking for, and was not willing to accept compromises.

During his twelve years in London, he never let any Grindr guy enter his apartment. He was paranoid that an unknown person could rob him, which happened to other people I know. The few times he had casual sex in a decade, it was at someone else's place. And it was not really sex as we consider it today.

Matthias was an extreme hypochondriac. There's a reason for that. When he moved here from Germany, he met a boy in a bar in Soho. They started going out, doing things together, and for a few months they've been meeting weekly. Sex with him was long and great. But on two occasions Matthias found out that the condom was totally broken after sex.

This may have happened, sex was wild and long, so Matthias bought thicker condoms and insisted on using more lubricant the following time. But, guess, the condom was broken again.

The next time they met and started to play, Matthias started to suck his cock and put the condom on with the tongue. While his ass being rimmed, he put a ton of lube over the boy's cock. He turned down on his stomach over the bed, and the boy went inside him. After half a second of penetration, Matthias pulled him out. And found out that the condom was broken again. It was him breaking the condom every time Matthias was having his head on the pillow.

Although the boy was denying the evidence, he finally admitted he was breaking condoms from the first time they met. He was allergic to latex, this was his justification. The condom was provoking him itches and scratches so he couldn't use it.

Matthias started to panic and told him he wanted to use protection, there are also condoms that are latex free, and they could try them. The boy agreed and left. But the following week, when they had to meet, he didn't show up.

Matthias went to a private hospital to test on all STDs and lived two weeks in hell while waiting for the results. He thought about the issue they were meeting only once a week. He was sure there was someone else in between, he was not his only partner. Paranoia was getting higher each day during these two weeks. Luckily, all the results were negative. But Matthias was never the same again.

He had no more confidence in people. He dreamt of a monogamous relationship that would end in a proposal for marriage on Primrose Hill one day. And he got so paranoid about fluids and potential diseases. He was living alone but was cleaning the toilet with disinfectants before and after the use.

For several years, his sexual life was confined to watching two porn DVDs bought in a sex shop in Soho. But he came to a point where he was missing the human touch. And since getting a hug was such a difficult job, and he didn't want to mix his body fluids with the people, he decided to play with fantasy.

On PlanetRomeo he discovered there are a lot of people with fetishes. One of the most common were feet. There were people willing to lick your feet while you're masturbating. No need to kiss, to suck, get sucked, or have any contact with body fluids. So when he was really desperate, let's say twice a year, not more, he was going to somebody's place for his toes to be licked while he was wanking and jerking off. This was giving him some small pleasure, with no risk at all. A good compromise for somebody that is afraid of any body fluids.

With Matthias, we had a lot in common. Not only we dreamed about monogamous relationships that were looking impossible to achieve. We were both agreeing we would never meet anything serious on Grindr, but we didn't know where else to look. He suggested that I should go to the Tate Modern on Sunday morning when all the bitches are sleeping, drunk or at some after-party. But I was too shy to approach someone live, didn't have any clue on how to do it. The whole world has gone online now, flirting as well. I'm really brave while sitting alone on my sofa with my mobile phone in my hands, but when it comes to a live approach, I'd just prefer to run away than starting to speak to some stranger randomly.

Although we never had anything together apart of deep friendship, he was the sign hat something better in life is possible. He was caring, in a city where nobody gives a shit about how you feel.

He was also my biggest supporter. To canalize loneliness and melancholy, I started to paint. I didn't have any technical background but was letting my feelings go out on the canvas. My paintings were the deepest expression of how life in London was for me. They were really transmitting my feeling of a lonely individual surrounded by other millions of people that didn't care. The few people that saw my painting loved them. I always thought I was not too good. When my self-esteem was the lowest ever, he contacted a few art galleries offering them my works. I told him he was crazy. We were in London and I was unknown and inexperienced. But thanks to his belief in me, some of my paintings were finally exposed and sold.

Another thing I liked to attach to my walls were vinyl stickers with positive messages, and we were passing hours at vintage markets looking for the best one.

We were two "strange bugs", he used to say, and together we were making our lives less hard through London's sense of loneliness and emptiness.

I'd also say our attitude was homophobic, at least somehow. We shared this sense of hate for the gay world. First of all, we didn't feel like being part of the gay community. Because what is the gay community? People that come together mainly with one thing in common: being gay.

We both thought that being gay was not our main property. We loved photography, theatre, he was an informatics freak, I loved to cook. So why not to call him a geek and me a cooking lover, instead of gay as a defining feature? I enjoyed much more interacting with people that were sharing some other passion of mine, no matter if they were gay or straight, than just being together with a gay, with the only thing in common for us being gay.

We were living in London, where gay people were well accepted. There was no need to close ourselves in a ghetto.

Also, the big majority of gay people we met were really superficial, promiscuous, were participating in orgies, fucking raw with whoever and at the same time lying to us they wanted a monogamous relationship, this to get what they wanted from us. We had too many experiences like that, that we started to mistrust anyone who was gay, just for the fact of being gay. We shared the hate for the community, for everything that was going around Soho Square. Because if everyone was behaving that way, this was precluding us from the possibility of finding, one day, what we desired: the possibility for a sincere, transparent and truly monogamous relationship to happen.

Matthias at least lived this experience once.

It was only after many years of knowing each other that I came to know his personal story, which was heavily dramatic. He was born in the surroundings of Munich, Germany, in a very conservative and patriarchal family. His father held a high range in the German military, and the rules at home had to be respected as if they were at the army barracks.

He found out he's gay very early. He fell in love with a boy at school, but there was no way of an acceptable coming out in the family. They loved each other. They were not actually planning to have a family and children, but definitely planned a life together.

The passion of Matthias was hospitality, and for getting the best possible education he needed to pass a few years studying in Leipzig, seeing his love only a few times a year. They knew this was the best for Matthias, it could give them a lot of opportunities for a future together, so they continued their relationship at a distance, in a time where WhatsApp or mobile phones were considered science fiction. They only had the landline phone, but there they couldn't speak freely. So they were intensely enjoying the few days per year together, waiting for the moment they would be in the same location, sharing their lives completely. Meanwhile, they were writing letters to each other.

As the best student of his generation, Matthias got the opportunity for an internship at the Adlon Hotel in Berlin, the most important place he could ever work in the country. More than an internship, this was a personalized specialization for a unique position in the whole of Germany, so who was chosen, was supposed to have a growing career inside the hotel.

When Matthias was living in Berlin, his boyfriend decided to make him a big surprise. Matthias didn't hear from his boyfriend for more than a week when he got a letter. "When you'll read this, I'll already be lying next to you in Berlin and you'll already know the whole story: I just packed my luggage and I'm ready to start the journey of my life. I'm coming to you now". It was a big surprise, but not bad at all. This is what they always wanted, and Berlin was the right place to start from scratch, a place where they could be anonymous professionals, with no military rules against them. But he was also worried. The letter was sent days ago, and the boyfriend had still not arrived.

It was just a few days later, during the weekly call Matthias was having with his mother, that she told him that a friend of his from school got into a car accident on a highway somewhere between Munich and Berlin, where he died.

His whole world has come down. He was feeling responsible for the death of the only person he loved.

Since it was only a friend from school, Hotel Adlon didn't give him permission to go to the funeral. He had an emotional breakdown and shortly lost his job.

Nobody in the world knew about their relationship.

And for Matthias, this was the first and last boy that ever loved him unconditionally.

When he moved to London he felt like I did: a mere piece of meat, somebody to have fun with in between of other two pieces of meat somebody was having fun with.

But differently from many of us, Matthias did feel the true reciprocate love, something that most people never do during their whole lifetime.

3. WITHOUT MATTHIAS

Matthias took away his life when I was on holiday in Thailand.

When I found that cheap flight to Asia, I invited him to join me. He was the right partner for this tropical trip and, differently from me, his employer was really flexible with holidays, so he could have come with me if he wanted.

The last time I saw him in my life was in a bar on Old Street, in the middle of my way from work to home. I had just broken up with Diego, my boyfriend, so going to Asia was a needed break. But for Matthias things were going much better than for me. For three months he was meeting with a boy, they were taking it slow, and it seemed to work. He got back the illusion and the faith in people, and he started to enjoy the moment but also got the courage to make life plans again after many years of isolation. I knew the boy, we had a lunch together a Sunday some months before in the food stall at Brick Lane, and he seemed to be cool. That boy is now fucking me hard and raw.

Matthias would have joined me in Thailand, but during my planned stay, he was invited to a barbecue with his boyfriend's friends in Southampton. It was the first time he was going to meet his friends, an important step for him, and he had already confirmed he'll be there for a whole weekend. He wanted to give himself the opportunity to build something meaningful, and that barbecue meant a lot to him.

I understood that. I felt very happy for him and decided to go to Thailand alone. I needed a break from the freezing grey weather, and wanted to stay as far as possible from my office, so a few days later I flew to Bangkok.

It was not a sexual holiday, I'm also not into Asian people, but being alone, at some point I got bored. One evening I was sitting alone at the 48 Garage bar in the old town of Chiang Mai, having a Leo beer, when I decided to open Grindr.

In my past travels through Asia I've found several people on Grindr that have shown me the city, in exchange for nothing, and I had a good time with them. During this trip I tried the same, but absolutely everyone was looking for sex, and sex now.

After blocking a few people insisting on meeting at my hotel, I was up to go home. I did a last refresh to the app when I saw I face I knew. His profile name was Scorpion, and he was my neighbor in London for at least a few years. I've never seen him live, but he was always online when I was opening the app at home.

Scorpion was a muscled Brazilian porn star, with a tattooed snake on his stomach. Definitely not the ideal husband for me, but since I like cinema and have seen a lot of his movies, having him a few meters away in London, I wrote him more than once when I was horny. He never replied.

Now he was 56 meters away, on the other side of the world. I wrote to him it was a too big coincidence to meet my neighbor in Chiang Mai, and that we definitely needed to meet.

He replied that he was already going to sleep, but we could meet at his hotel, the Akara Lanna, the following afternoon. So the next day, after visiting a few temples and the Warorot market in the East of the city, I headed to Scorpion's hotel.

Although we never spoke about having sex, I've never been with a porn star before, as far as I know it, and I was excited to try it. When the cab let me two blocks away from his hotel, he wrote me a message saying that his room was busy, so we should meet in the hotel's public toilet, just left of the entrance.

Next to a motorbike rental on Ratchapakhinai road, there was a thin paved path leading to the hotel, which was one of the most luxurious places in central Chiang Mai. I entered the courtyard, went to the left and found the toilets. The doors looked like a Texas saloon door, so you could see who's in the toilet. The first one was empty, and in the second one, I could see two tanned muscular legs, feet wearing flip-flops.

I opened the saloon door, and there he was him, in flesh and blood. There was a lot of blood in the cock, actually, since he was hard, waiting for me. No words, I put myself on my knees and started to suck Scorpion's member, the one I've seen being sucked so many times in the movies I was looking online when I was at home.

I was the star now. I was enjoying it, at the beginning slowly with my tongue, later going faster and harder, and harder. Too hard at some point, since I've felt the taste of blood in my mouth, put his cock away and panicked. I was convinced his cock was the one bleeding, but he has shown me it was my upper lip that got broken.

I couldn't continue, so we both jerked off inside the toilet. I told him I was very worried, he reassured me that he was ok, whatever that meant. After washing our hands in the lavatory and getting dressed, he invited me to his terrace, facing one of the best swimming pools in town.

He was not alone at the hotel, though. He stayed there with his husband. For me there was no problem, we could have a drink together. I was alone, and it would be nice to have a chat with someone, so I accepted.

The man sitting at the terrace was at least seventy years old, with a big belly, falling breasts and an orange peel skin. He was very eloquent, though. They told me they came to Thailand to sell one of their houses in Pattaya, and they stopped for a few more days because they both loved Thai guys. The old man was extremely rich, I'm sure he was a retired politician or retired businessman. And married to a young Brazilian porn star. He was proudly sharing information with me about the saunas in Bangkok's Silom district, where you can fuck some young Thai boy for a branch of pounds. I felt disgusted and didn't have sexual contact with anyone for a while after that.

Back in London, months later, I've found Scorpion advertising himself on Grindr as an escort, offering exclusively raw fuck services. The cock I was having in my mouth in Thailand barebacked hundreds of London's old asses.

When I was leaving the Thai Akara Lanna, I checked my phone and found a WhatsApp message from Matthias.

EUSTON, WE HAVE A PROBLEM

"Why is everyone always the same? Why? Why?"

The message had been sent two hours before. I replied to him, asking what happened, but my message was not delivered. I thought it must be because of the time zone. I supposed he was sleeping and so his phone was switched off.

Since the following day the message was still not delivered, I tried to call him, although the intercontinental cost of the call, but his phone was still off. I guessed he was having a big crisis, probably with the boy he was dating, and he decided to have a total disconnection for a few days. I wrote him an email message, saying I was here for anything he needed, but he didn't reply either. He was used to dealing with big shit alone, so I supposed this time he decided to keep it all for himself, in search of a solution.

Three days later I became worried. I was at Suvarnabhumi airport, boarding the plane back to London, when I sent him another email, asking me to reassure me he was ok. When I landed in London the following day there was still no reply.

Only at that point, I discovered we didn't know each other very well. We didn't have any friends in common.

In the late afternoon I went to his flat, rang the door, but nobody answered. I waited there for a few hours, sitting on the stairs outside of his building, but he didn't appear.

There was one thing I knew, almost by accident: his surname. He gave it to me when I needed to buy our tickets for a show in Leicester Square. Back home, at night I googled his name and surname, filtered by date last week, but nothing appeared in the search.

My brain was trying to find a justification for his absence. Maybe he took holidays and went back to Germany, to his family, for a while. I hadn't had any contact with his family during all the years we've been friends, and I had no clue about how to find them. I've never been to the hotel he was working at, but this was my last chance to find out where he was.

"He died", told me the receptionist with the same tone as she would say that it was raining today. On my insistence, she told me she was not allowed to give more details. GPDR, she alleged coldly.

No letter explaining why he did it. I should have seen that Matthias was not ok. He seemed the strongest of the two. I was always complaining to him about my experiences, crying in his arms and he was always finding the energy to take me out of situations I've been deep into. He kept a lot for himself, probably too much to deal with all that shit alone.

I'm sure what happened was connected to the boy he was dating, and he was going to have a barbecue with in Southampton. But, I can only wonder what happened and will never know it. I've made a few theories, all connected with that boy. The one I'm now sucking on my sofa, and doesn't even recognize me although we had lunch a few times together with Matthias.

His cock in my mouth is becoming the most bitter thing I've ever tried.

I'm disgusted. I crossed the line.

I pull the cock out of my mouth. I want to vomit.

I try to go to the bathroom.

I stand up on my legs, but I can't make it. I just fall down, with my face on the bed.

4. PAWEL

Back in the Nineties, in the province, when I found out I was gay, it was almost impossible to speak about it with anyone. There was a national chat website, with a lot of chat rooms. One of these rooms was for gays. Only nicknames, no photos, almost all the people were from the capital or other big cities. There were also skinheads and extremists, trying to insult, someone even to meet live and hurt physically the ones that were gay.

The first time I acceded, I was scared. There was a public gay room where people were leaving public messages, but you could also speak with any of the users in the room privately, opening a private chat window.

After a few months of going in and out that orange-colored chat, without even having more than two sentences with anyone, I've seen a profile called "gay-love" and started to speak to him. He was not speaking about sex, like all the others, so I used the opportunity to make him basic questions, trying to understand what was going on with me.

I was connecting every afternoon after school, waiting for him to be online, which was normally happening in the evenings. He was living in Warsaw and working in IT. I remember that emotion seeing him entering into the chat. We were speaking about life, I was confessing to him my innocent feelings, and through the months I've completely fallen in love with him. Nowadays that would sound crazy, but I never saw a photo of him. I could imagine how he was looking just by his description: 1,85 cm high, slim, intelligently bold, green eyes, and some details like that. In my imagination, he was the cutest boy in the world. I've never thought about his cock. I was feeling in love with him for what he was saying.

I was ready to invent any excuse to tell my parents and go to the capital to meet him, but he was avoiding it. He was present, giving me strong emotional support, but he was not willing to meet me.

The moment we met was one of the most awkward situations in my life. If I read this in a book, I would never believe something like that could happen.

My school won a national project promoted by the Department for Education, and some of the students were invited to the capital to present it. I was among the lucky ones. While in Warsaw, I was insisting to him that we needed to meet. At that time we already exchanged our phone numbers, got only a few calls, done secretly, from a park or in the wild countryside. We were mostly exchanging SMS messages, something pretty expensive for a student at that time. The fact is that I was bothering him so much that he finally accepted to meet me.

We were a group of four students and three teachers visiting Warsaw. After the presentation, our geography teacher, who had finished her studies in the capital, took us to a restaurant where they serve the best fried chicken meat in town. Hours before, I already informed my English teacher that after dinner a friend was going to pick me up and take me to have a short drink. I was a minor, so I told the teacher that my parents knew him very well, and we'd be back at the hotel soon. Since I was a good student, I was shy and reliable, she didn't suspect it could be a lie.

But fate wanted our meeting to be something we'll remember forever. While having dinner, I bit my tongue and a few drops of blood started to drip. I put some paper wipes in my mouth, and when I took them out, they were red. I was really feeling no pain but was feeling panic. I needed to meet the supposed love of my life, or at least the first gay boy I've ever met in my life, in less than half an hour. I didn't want my teacher to keep me at the hotel because of my tongue.

We took the tram back to the hotel, and the teacher insisted on seeing my tongue. It was not bleeding anymore. I said I was ok, that everything was fine, but she insisted on seeing it. There was a cut, and she told me we needed to go to the hospital, because she was my legal tutor during that trip, and she didn't want me to die choked by my own blood in a hotel. I wanted to meet him but I knew she'll not let me go to the meeting, so I said ok, and told her I would have called my friend to cancel the meeting.

Still in the tram, the geography teacher told is that the otolaryngology hospital was far away, and the English teacher said there was no problem: since my friend was coming to see me, he could take us to the hospital. All in panic, I started to say no, no, no. If I could not meet him alone, I would call him and cancel the meeting.

But as an innocent kid who just discovered he was gay, I was thinking everyone around me knew I was panicking because of Pawel, this was his name.

We left the tram, and when we arrived in front of the hotel, I told the teacher I'll stay on the street to call my friend.

I called my first love telling him what the teacher was proposing, and he told me he was sorry, but in that case he was heading back home. I told him about my lie to the teacher, and that she was still expecting him to come pick me up. I was feeling awkward, but after all, this was still an opportunity to see him for the first time. He said he had a red Renault Clio and would arrive to the hotel in a few minutes. I asked him to act as we knew each other for a long time.

Me and the teacher waiting on the street, a red Renault Clio parked just in front of us. An elderly man, with no hair at all and ears looking like a Star Wars character said: "Hi, Adam". The teacher and I entered the red Renault Clio, and my friend started to make small talk. "How long no see you", "are you ok?", "how is your family?", these typical questions not to show we don't know each other at all. The only thing I was thinking at that moment was that my teacher could suspect that we were gay.

We arrived at the urgencies and I was received immediately by a female doctor. Meanwhile, my teacher and my first love were sitting together in the waiting room. The doctor told me she should put me points on the wound, but since the wound was so small, and it would be hurtful, she wanted to try to heal it with sterile gauze before.

With sterile gauze in my mouth, I was wondering what the other two were speaking about in the waiting room.

I was also thinking of how ugly he was, and I was sure he lied to me about his age, but I still loved him a lot. There are not a lot of gay boys in Poland, I thought, and this one is so kind, nice, empathic and understanding with me for months, so I wanted to get to know him much more. I already dreamt about how his house was, never thought of living together, that was so gay, and not normal in a conservative environment like ours, but I hoped to come soon to the capital again and, after school, to live in the same city as him.

The doctor asked me to open my mouth, she decided that the wound was healed, no need for points, so I could leave.

Pawel drove us back to the hotel and since it was very late and we were traveling the next morning, I said him goodbye, see you soon, and entered the hotel with my teacher. In the elevator, with a tone of amusement, the teacher told me that my friend was such a nice person. During the hour they were waiting for me, she had a lot of fun. Long story short, my first gay date ever was actually a date between a boy I met on chat with my English teacher.

Needless to say, I didn't sleep that night. Finally, I've met him. But I was also scared. What will my teacher think? Did she get that I was in love with him? And how will Pawel react? I felt I was doing something wrong, that was not morally accepted, something almost illegal. And I still didn't even have my first kiss.

Fortunately, he was so understanding and we continued to stay in contact. He reassured me there was no reason that the teacher could think I was gay because of meeting with him. Months later, we met again. Since I did not have a lot of money to pay for accommodation, he acceded to host me for a weekend at his home, but he told me clearly we were not going to have sex. I lied to my parents I was going to visit some friends in the capital and, since I was a reliable boy, they didn't doubt my words either. Pawel came to pick me up at the bus station, we went to a supermarket and cooked dinner at his home. I was speaking like a torrent, about my doubts and scares, he was telling me about his life experiences with other men, and he was sounding like a really frustrated person. He was still in love with his ex-boyfriend. They broke up after on many occasions money was missing from home. After the breakup, he discovered that his boyfriend was selling his body around for a bunch of Polish Zloty. Stories like that were, for an innocent boy coming from a rural province like me, science fiction. I could not believe this could happen anywhere in the world, much less in my country.

But I got one thing very clear: the gay world was a fucked up place, and I had in front of me a difficult road to walk through.

We were supposed to watch a movie or have a walk through the city center, but my need to speak to someone like me, that understands me, that I can share my doubts for the first time in my life, went into till deep night, so we just went to sleep.

He kissed me in the cheeks and I asked if I could hug him. He said of course. And I did. We were wearing pajamas but I could feel his hot body, and my heartbeat was becoming faster and faster. I couldn't sleep, I was feeling happy, feeling safe. I was touching his defined hairy belly and I loved it. I moved my hand over his nipples.

I was discovering somebody else's body for the first time.

Given my heartbeat and my hands over his body, he also couldn't sleep, but he was acting like he was sleeping hard. I wanted to explore deeper, but I was scared. My hand was going around his belly for a really long time until I found the courage to go lower. Initially, I touched him over the pajamas, and his cock was really,

really big and hard as a rock. He was still acting to be asleep, so after some more time, I've been so brave to pull his pajamas down and touch it through the slips he was wearing. Still acting he's asleep, he moved my hand away, and I started from zero: hugs, belly, nipples, belly again, this time coming down and pulling directly down his slips. I was touching his cock with no barriers, for the first time. I remember my hand moving up and down the skin of his uncut cock. He loved it, and enjoyed it a lot. He had much more experience than me, but he was enjoying my innocence, the purity of a person that is exploring the unknown, slowly discovering the pleasure, and is finding a way to be brave enough to do something for the first time. I put my hand in my mouth, licked my fingers, and went back to his uncut skin, up and down. It lasted a while, I was feeling his pleasure and I loved it. At some point, with a sad voice, he asked me to stop. He told me he was much older than the age he had told me in the chat. I already knew he was not 28, but I didn't want to stop exploring this mystery that was another person's body.

He insisted that, although he liked me a lot, he didn't want to abuse me. And he was sincere, not because I was still a minor, but because he wanted me to have my first experience in the best possible way, something good to remember, and he didn't want to take away my innocence from me.

Pawel is the first person I've ever kissed. I put my tense inexperienced tongue inside his mouth, moving it around with all my strength. It was the most aggressive kiss I've ever given. Fortunately, he was patient enough and a good teacher, and he took his time to make me learn to slow down and enjoy the moment. Thanks to him, I became a great kisser. And there's a lot of people out there, even in their late forties, that are kissing as aggressively as I was the first time.

EUSTON, WE HAVE A PROBLEM

We've been in contact for all the years I stayed in Poland, sometimes we passed a weekend together. Looking back, I've been lucky enough to find a person that really respected me and cared about me. We even had sex once, a very pleasant one, many years later during a holiday in Spain together.

Not all has gone so great with him, although. After that first weekend together at his home, I was more in love with him than I was before. He was actually the only gay person I knew. I'd not say I became obsessed with him, but he was a reference to everything. And he was part of my plans for the future. After school, I planned to move to Warsaw to study, but this was an excuse. I could study wherever else, but in Warsaw I'd have the opportunity to know him better, maybe to develop something. I would not even be a minor anymore, so there shouldn't have been any technical or legal problems either.

But he was less innocent than me, doubling my age, with stress at work and physical needs. Since the national gay chat was one of the few places to meet people, I saw him coming online many evenings. He was kind to me, always responding to my messages with empathy, and also taking all my phone calls in the evenings. But he was still there, on the chat. And more than once wished me a good night already at 9 PM. I knew he was meeting other people, he was having sex with them. And, until that time, he never wanted to have it with me. I was asking myself if I was too ugly or too fat. I started to feel very insecure and didn't have anyone else to speak to.

One evening I saw him coming online in the chat room as many other times. He replied to all my messages and at some point, he sent his goodnight message and disappeared. At the time, there was an option on the SMS messages, and maybe it still exists: the notification of delivery of a message. This service was having a cost, so most people were having it off, not to spend double the money for all their messages. I turned the service on. It was around 11 PM. I sent him a message and saw it was not delivered, which was logical since he was supposed to sleep and probably had the mobile phone switched off. I was staring at the black and green screen of my Nokia 3210 for about two and a half hours, waiting for the message to be delivered, but the status was not changing from "pending". At 1:30 PM, when I was about to go to sleep, I got the delivery notification.

His mobile phone was off when he was having sex, so if someone like me called, he wouldn't be disturbed. He turned it on just after his fuck buddy left. I started to shiver, and felt a strange cold inside my body. I felt a strong sense of impotence and, at some point, I couldn't breathe anymore.

It was my first panic attack ever.

Like the one I'm having tonight.

5. HOT LIQUID

I'm lying down breathless on my bed, and someone's over me, riding my ass strongly.

I cannot move my head, but I guess who's behind. In front of me, there are three blokes. One of them, with open legs on the kitchen table, is getting his ass rimmed by Frank, which seems to be back again and which is being sucked by a young slim guy that I've never seen before, so he may have joined in the last minutes. The slim guy is lying under the table, licking Frank's horse cock and alternating it with a speech about animal cruelty in the fashion industry, but nobody is actually listening to him.

Whoever is behind me, he's riding me too strongly, and even on anesthetic drugs, I feel pain.

I don't know for how much time is all of this lasting, but it seems it will never end.

I would like to ask for help, but no voice is coming out of me. I feel powerless. And he's riding me faster and faster.

The moment he starts screaming of pleasure, I'm sure. I'm getting fucked by Matthias' last boyfriend. And the scream coincides with him slowing down as well as a hot liquid entering inside me.

I stay still, motionless, and at that moment I'm thrown in the past, to the moment when, for the first time, I've felt that same hot liquid inside me and I've felt disgusted and dirty the same as tonight.

6. OLEK

It was at the time I was going to the gay chat room every evening to check if my Warsaw love will be there. One evening a user joined the room and, in the public chat, asked if there was someone from my city.

So there were gays in my city too, I thought. I was an enthusiast. My town had about sixty thousand people, but in my mind, I was the only gay there. Until that moment I saw this boy appearing in the chat room.

I opened a private chat with him, and we exchanged a few messages. He was 34, working as a DJ, and he was willing to meet immediately. I told him I had no experience. Although I was scared as fuck, I was actually willing to meet him and speak, if he wanted. I didn't think about having sex, also because I was madly in love with the older boy from Warsaw. I was looking for a friend, someone to speak to about forbidden topics, someone to explain to me how things worked in this world and to reassure me I was not the only one here.

That evening I was 17 years and 11 months old. My parents were on holidays, and the house was all for me, so I thought about inviting him to have a drink. On these chats, there was no possibility to exchange files, only text messages, so in case you wanted to see someone's photo, you needed to exchange email addresses. We didn't do that. I gave him my home address, and he told me he was leaving immediately to my place with his motorbike, he would ring my bell in less than 5 minutes.

I was still shocked. Five minutes before I've just met someone in the chat room, he was from my city, and he was going to be at my home in 5 minutes only. I didn't give myself the time to even imagine what he would look like, didn't know anything about him, his interests, apart from his age and that he was a music DJ.

I can still hear the noise of his motorbike stopping in front of my door. Me trembling from the other side, waiting for him to ring, scared of whom I was going to find when I'd opened the door but also worried that some of the neighbors could see him going in, or could see his motorbike in front of my house, or even that some friends of my parents could come to visit while he's in.

I can't remember him entering the house. What I remember is us in the living room, me serving two small glasses of Jägermaister, or maybe it was Bailey's, while he was sitting on the sofa speaking about a friend of his, I still remember her name, Katarina. Can't say if we spoke for a minute or for two hours. The next thing I can remember is him opening his pants, pulling his cock out from some vintage underwear and me sucking it, without any pleasure, without even wanting it. But this was the first cock I sucked. It made me think that maybe I was not even gay, I didn't like that cock at all.

I remember his hot cum inside me, but this didn't happen on the same evening. During the month following our first meeting, we continued to see each other. His name was Aleksandar, Olek, for friends. Although he didn't lie about his age, he was doubling mine, he lied about his job. He was working as a bartender in the only gym in town. He told me we were a couple now, although because of secrecy it didn't look so. I didn't feel comfortable with him, so I decided to break up with him on my 18th birthday. I will never forget that night.

The day before my birthday he already gave me a birthday card, signed as "Olek, the failed DJ", which meant he wanted to be a DJ but ended up working frustratedly in a bar. On the day of my birthday, I went to the gym where he was working and told him I was not feeling comfortable continuing the so-called relationship. He was not ok with it, but let me go.

The surprise arrived at midnight on my birthday in the form of an SMS, with a content that for an 18 year old boy was really scary. The message was saying he was killing himself at that moment. I panicked. I tried to convince him not to do it, but any of his following messages was less understandable than the one before. I felt the responsibility of his life on me.

I was not used to leaving my house late at night, especially without my parents knowing it. They were asleep and the only possibility I thought of saving him was to go to his flat. He was also living with his parents and one sister. When I told him I was going to see him, he agreed, surprisingly. When I reached the building, he opened the door and let me in. We were in the same flat as his family sleeping. Once in his room, I asked him how he planned to kill himself, and he showed me some pills blisters and told me he had already taken all of them, so it was already all over.

I was naive and innocent and never heard about people killing themselves with pills until that moment. But I saw that his reflections had slowed down and the only thing I thought was taking him to the bathroom and checking that he throws the pills out. And so I did. Before I left, he asked me to promise him I was not going to leave him, treating me he would kill himself if I did it.

On the way back home, I was out of myself. A lot of questions arose. What is one of his parents woke up while I was making him throw the pills in the toilet? What if he died in front of me and his family found me? What should I do now? But first of all, a thought: someone was trying to kill himself because of me, and I was responsible for this.

I was just a child, I was legally an adult for about two hours, and already got a heavy load on my soul. And, worst of all, I couldn't share it with anybody. I felt as I was alone in the world and didn't know what to do.

I continued to see Olek for about a month. But it was not voluntary, it was all based on a threat. One day I decided I can't handle such heavy load anymore, I had to think about myself surviving, and I disappeared, letting him do what he thought was the best for him.

He never killed himself. I haven't heard from him ever since, but one summer some fifteen years later I was walking through my hometown and saw him serving beers on the terrace of a pub.

I remember Olek because of the hot cum inside my ass. He was the first one to enter inside me, although I couldn't say we ever made love. Worst, we didn't have a proper penetration that lasted even for a few minutes.

During the month we were "dating", both of us didn't have a place to meet, both were living with our parents, and he was insisting on having complete sex, saying he wanted to feel his body inside me.

As an inexperienced boy from the countryside, I thought all gays have AIDS. This was at least what I heard from other people before. And I didn't even know there was a difference between HIV and AIDS. I've just heard that AIDS was a sickness that all gays were having and were dying of. I was ignorant, and Olek reassured me that he had no AIDS. This was a sickness that people in big American cities had, nobody had it in our small town. He was more ignorant than me, however, for some years, I've connected HIV only with big Western capitals. And I was totally wrong.

So one evening he let me inside his building, and took me to the elevator. We went to the basement floor. This was the place he had chosen to take away my virginity. Surrounded by the smell of cellars and no light on. He asked me to pull down my pants. My sweater and shoes were still on. Then he started wanking behind me. At the moment he was up to cum, he entered inside me with full power, no lubricants, and let his hot fluid enter inside me.

After he cum, he said it was great and he put his pants up. He called the elevator, and let me at the entrance door, wishing me a good night and going back to his flat.

I felt awkward, like a hole where to discharge someone's leftovers. This was definitely not the love life I always dreamt about. I was feeling dirty, uncomfortable, everything was so mechanical, no feelings, no consent. I've somehow been raped. And I thought that being gay meant it would always be like that.

The penetration with Oleg was, of course, with no condom. Back home at night, I went online with my 56K modem, the one that was making these strange sounds over the phone line, to search for information. Google was still not founded. The search engine at the time was Altavista, and Wikipedia was still not even in plans. So I didn't find much information to be reassured.

My life andfuture have been marked in a dark, smelly basement, hidden from the world, like we've been doing something wrong, illegal.

Considering my painful first time, there's nothing strange that for the following ten years I was only a top, and didn't let anyone enter there again.

7. DIRTY FEELINGS

Until tonight, at a chemsex party, I've never had a panic attack. Chemsex has been for me a safe place where I was feeling comfortable, my way of escaping from my gray and lonely day to day and the real world.

Here I was always getting all the attention I needed, the physical contact I missed. Now I just cannot move, I can not even say a word.

People around me are continuing to enjoy, nobody is noticing I'm not ok.

Three of them are on the same sofa as me, having some action. One gets angry and starts to argue with another: "How can you say that the Red Cross was allied with the Nazis? My grandma was working with the Red Cross in Switzerland during the Second World War and she personally saved tens of lives". The other bloke puts him his cock in the mouth, and the arguer starts to suck him, as the discussion of half a second before never happened.

I feel like I have been raped. But am I? I'm in my house, I voluntarily let this man enter here, I was naked when he arrived, I was sucking his cock before and, most important of all, I haven't even asked him to stop.

It is true, I was on drugs. But he is probably like me.

He's dressing and leaving. He was here for a short time, just to empty his balls before sleeping.

I feel dirty and disgusting. I've just been fucked by the boy that Matthias took his life away for.

And I remember it's not the first time I feel I've been raped, and I feel dirty.

A few years ago I've bought a ticket for a concert in Milan, and I've bought the flights, but I was not able to find accommodation. There was a tourism fair, and the few rooms left were too overpriced. So I used CouchSurfing. A guy called Vincenzo hosted me in his flat, not far from the fashion triangle. I met him in the afternoon, left my luggage at his place, and went to the concert.

When I was back, we had a glass of wine together and we went to sleep in two separate beds, although in the same room. In the middle of the night, I've been woken up by him touching my cock. I tried to push him away, but he insisted. I told him I didn't want it to continue, but he didn't stop. I wanted to leave, but outside there was heavy rain, all the hotels were overbooked, and I had no clue where else to go. After some time trying to reject him, I let him do what he wanted. After I jerked off, he asked me what time I was waking up to catch my flight. He woke up half an hour before that and woke me up again sucking my cock for the second time. I didn't even try to stop him, I knew it would have been useless. This time when I jerked off, he asked me: "did you really think you'll stay at my place for free?"

He was cute, I would have even fucked with him spontaneously if it would have happened naturally. But as he did, I was forced to do it. And it was not pleasant at all.

An even worse experience I had on CouchSurfing happened in Borneo, during a trip through Malaysia. There, the accommodation is so cheap, so I was not for looking a place to sleep, but just for someone to have a beer with after I passed a full week alone in the jungle. I published a public announcement looking for someone to share a beer with, but I never had any beer.

I was contacted by a Muslim guy who doesn't drink alcohol. He offered to show me his city and he drove me up and down the Sarawak region with his car. The environment in Malaysia is too conservative, so I never told him I was gay, nor did he tell me anything about his sexual life. The following day he invited me to the cinema and then to have dinner with his brother and sister at a halal restaurant. The topics at the dinner were so conservative, I could never imagine he was gay. He was actually really good looking, I'd not discard a shag with him, but being in Malaysia, I could also survive without it.

At dinner, he insisted that I leave my hostel. It was better if I slept at their house, so his brother could take me to the airport early in the morning. I initially denied it, but the whole family was excited to have a guest at home, so I went with them.

Their house was one of the richest places I've seen in Asia. There were three floors, with big glass windows. After we all watched a bit of Malaysian TV on the ground floor, they showed me my room. I was sleeping alone with a cat, on the ground floor, and everyone else was sleeping somewhere upstairs. I thanked everyone for their hospitality and we all went to sleep.

I woke up in the middle of the night, the CouchSurfing guy sitting on me, my hard cock just entered raw inside him. Sexual contact lasted one second, but my paranoia arose over the following three months. In a conservative environment like Malaysia, gay people are not accepted, so they also don't get tested.

Like many other times in my life, I was lucky and STD free.

But Asia gave me another experience, scarier than this one.

It was during the same trip, on Palawan Island, in the Philippines. I've been passing a few days with a group of straight friends in El Nido, which is also known for being surrounded by an archipelago of virgin islands, one of the last paradises on Earth. It was our last night there, the biggest typhoon of the year was on its way, and we all needed to escape to somewhere safer the next day.

Although it is very touristic, El Nido has only one place to go out at night. It is a bamboo hut located right away on the beach, called Pukka Bar, where they play reggae music, and everyone is there. I went to Pukka Bar with three Australian girls. We've been drinking San Miguel beer and dancing when a boy appeared on what was supposed to be the dance floor and started to shake his ass around me. I stayed in hostels for weeks and didn't have the opportunity to jerk off properly, so I immediately got hard. My friend Carlie pushed me into him, and we kissed. His tongue made me even harder, and he was hard too. So I just looked at him and we left the place together.

Five meters out of the bar, with all the lights and people upstairs, we started to take off our clothes. We moved another twenty meters north, found a paved path between two houses, I put on a condom and started to fuck him. I loved it, and also needed it, I didn't have proper sex for months, and he seemed to enjoy it too. A few seconds before I was up to jerk off he said: "it's five hundred". I stopped, took my cock outside of him, and said no. He was a prostitute and wanted five hundred pesos to be fucked. I started to shake. Five hundred pesos is less than eight pounds, it was not for the money. Prostitution in the Philippines is common, but I refused to pay because he didn't tell me he was a prostitute before we started to fuck. At that point, he told me he was a minor, and if I don't pay him, he'd have called the police. I told him I was going to call the police if he didn't disappear, and I left. But he was following me, screaming to me that the police woul fuck me up. And he was right, in these places the police are normally partners in crime with prostitutes. The Italian ambassador in Manila Daniele Bosio knows something about that. He passed a few months in jail after a situation like the one I was living now. On the way to my hotel, him following me, we were both screaming at each other. A French friend of mine, Aline, heard my screams from her terrace and came down to the street to ask what was going on. Luckily, at that moment the boy got scared and ran away.

I've been thinking a lot about this guy. I don't blame him. Getting eight pounds from a tourist was the only job he could have as gay in that small village. But that night I felt dirty. I had the longest shower ever and went to bed. I cried and shook for a while, and needed a second shower, then a third one.

Now, on my sofa, I feel the same dirt. And I'm not able to ask for help.

Maybe it is not only a panic attack. I may have gone to overdose.

But of what

ADAM KACZINSKY

8. CHEMS

If it's not the biggest panic attack I've ever had, if I have really gone to overdose, what drug could it be?

As people going out to dance in clubs were taking cocktails, participating in a chemsex meant taking a cocktail too. For the *party and play* to be good, for being fucking high and horny for days, the cocktail that was letting us enjoy was a mix of crystal meth, mephedrone, and GHB.

To lose any inhibition, feel awake, high and exhilarated I needed crystal meth, which we also call Tina. This is a powder that is usually snorted, but it can also be smoked through a glass pipe. It was originally used by bikers and truckers to stay awake on long journeys. Thanks to crystal meth, I could feel super horny and could dance naked in front of a group of men I didn't know without feeling uncomfortable. Also sexually, I could do stuff I'd normally be ashamed of. It was giving me energy, making me feel confident, almost invincible. And it was also anesthetic: I didn't feel any pain when doing anything. It was also pushing up my heartbeat, making me feel really excited. But, best of all, Tina was stopping me from coming. I could enjoy sex for hours without jerking off. The high of crystal meth lasts between four and twenty-four hours, depending on how much you take. Meth makes you feel good for long periods and you might go days without eating or sleeping.

But to really get horny'n'highy, meth alone is not enough.

To get really stimulated, feel euphoric, alert, and feel a deep affection for the people that are around us, there is Mephedrone, a powerful amphetamine synthetic stimulant that makes you feel quite talkative, and makes you even hornier. You can swallow it or snort it. Some people are also injecting it, but I didn't let anyone do it at my place: sharing needles with other people could put us at high risk of getting hepatitis C. Meth it is extremely popular and totally inexpensive. It's effect is similar to that of MDMA. Meph was legal unttil 2010, when it was banned due to the number of deaths linked to it. The only meph's effect I didn't like at the beginning was that it was making me sweat like honey. But I came to like and enjoy that group sweating too.

With all the high of meth and meph, to have a crazy weekend full of sex with strangers, there's the need for something that slows you down, a downer.

And the best towner is GHB or its variant GBL, also called G, a depressant drug that slows your body and its functions down. It not only makes you horny but also gives you a total sense of relaxation. And if you need to take a load of big cocks in your arse, you don't feel any pain. G comes as a clear, salty liquid with no smell that's usually mixed with a soft drink. Doses are often measured with eye drops, small syringes or a capful. When you use it regularly, your body starts to tolerate more of the drug, and you can take one capful every few hours.

The high of G comes on after about twenty minutes and lasts for about one hour only. But it makes you feel so chilled out, fucking horny and mildly high. We normally use it to boost the effects of the other chems, but also to boost sexual desire, since it also makes you feel euphoric, with a loss of inhibitions, increased confidence and a higher sex drive.

One thing I love about chems, they make sex easier. From a physical point of view, they are enabling a great level of relaxation, which is very helpful during anal sex.

Although the ejaculation with all these drugs is always delayed, one side effect of crystal meth is what we call crystal dick, stopping the member from getting a hard-on. But there is an easy solution, using a legal pill that can be bought at a pharmacy: Who hasn't heard of Viagra today?

Another legal thing we are almost all taking is PrEP, which is meant to protect us from HIV contagion.

Gym-addicted blokes also usually take muscle building anabolic steroids to get their bodies pumped up.

Some people coming to visit are also snorting cocaine. I have to say coke is not a basic drug for doing chems. As for our chems, cocaine also makes you feel confident, euphoric, alertness, invincible and all-conquering, but it is also much more expensive than the other drugs, so it is mostly used by short-time visitors that are not taking much of the other substances.

A few people are also using ketamine, since it has the power to put you into a trippy, trance-like state and its aesthetic qualities, so there is no pain in the arse.

I never took keta. At one of the first horny and high parties, I hosted in my flat one boy got an overdose. We were a group of people fucking on the sofa when we noticed him unconscious on my bed, surrounded by vomit. Someone suggested calling emergency services, but this was not an option. We were all on drugs, Frank was having a full backpack of stuff here, and it was all happening inside my flat. Possession of drugs can get you up to two years of prison and an unlimited fine. For supplying it, you could be imprisoned for up to fourteen years. There was no way of calling emergency services, they would also notify the police.

I've been into a police station only once, at Paddington Green near Edgware Road Station. It was when the stupid CCTV caught me pissing on the street at night. It was a human need, and I ended up paying fucking five hundred pounds for it. I was not going to see a police station again, especially not going there for possession (or even supplying) of drugs.

So me and two mates dressed up and put clothes on the fainted bloke. I remember he was as heavy as a millstone. We struggled to take him down the stairs to Eversholt Street, then took him a few doors away from mine and went back to the party. I suppose he was okay. The next morning we went to check, and he was not there, so I'm sure he got better or he got help, and I didn't have any problems with justice.

Apart from all the chems we are taking, most of the people that are regulars at chemsex parties have an extremely healthy lifestyle. I'd say they are taking care of their bodies and health. I discovered that most of them are vegetarians, someone even vegan, eating organic raw food and regularly going to the gym.

Before I started to host parties at my place, I have been refused by some people because I was a smoker. Apart from being smelly, it was unhealthy, I was told. And although I've unsuccessfully tried to stop smoking for years, I was never able to. Until I started with chemsex. Before that, I was considering cigarettes as my only friend, as a great company in all situations of life. But the possibility of creating a new social life with a much bigger company, feeling like a real community, was enough motivation to stop.

Now that I am unable to move, I start to clearly see how many drugs I've been regularly putting inside my body together. Meth, meph, GHB, Viagra, PrEP... How could my liver bear all of this together?

It is a miracle that I am still alive.

And I'm starting to remember what I read about these drugs through the years, but somehow my brain has decided to erase it completely.

Crystal meth pushes up body temperature, heartbeat and blood pressure, possibly to dangerous levels, with a risk of heart attack, stroke, coma or, in less lucky cases, death. Come-downs can leave a person feeling exhausted, aggressive, paranoid and, in some cases, even suicidal. Depending on how crystal meth is taken, it can damage the lungs, nose, and mouth. It can also provoke agitation, paranoia and confusion, to the point of psychosis. As its effects last for so long, people can forget to take their HIV treatment or PrEP.

Meph also provokes anxiety and paranoia, as well as strong headaches, vomiting, insomnia and teeth grinding. As a vascular constrictor, it narrows the veins and makes the heart pump faster. The comedown that follows the high can be horrific. This is because meth causes an enormous surge of dopamine in the brain, and dopamine is what makes you feel euphoria and sexual arousal. The pleasure is enhanced, the sexual boundaries disappear, you're a social butterfly. But when the dopamine is over, all those feelings disappear, taking you back to the emptiness you had before, but much stronger.

But the worst consequences can happen when taking GHB, also known as Satan's urine. It is very easy to overdose on G, and you can enter into a GHB-induced coma, which also leaves you vulnerable to being sexually assaulted. A slightly greater dose can even lead to a respiratory collapse and death. If mixed with other drugs and alcohol, the adverse risks are multiplied. GHB is physically addictive and is almost impossible to stop taking it without medical assistance. Too much G leaves you dizzy, drowsy or vomiting, and that vomit could also cause death if you're knocked out by G.

And although I never overdosed, I experienced many of these consequences. But my brain didn't want to see it, I always wanted to think that there's no risk at all. Being surrounded by people was too good, and I didn't want to think there may be any adverse effects.

Also, all these three chems lower your inhibitions, making you at risk for passing on HIV, syphilis, herpes, gonorrhea, etc.

And this is what I now have. Gonorrhea.

9. GONORRHEA

I am holding a chemsex at home this weekend, but I got diagnosed with gonorrhea earlier this week.

Although I lost the scar to all STDs, every few months I go for a medical checkup. I do it because in 2016 there has been a case in Canada where a guy got HIV while on PrEP. It is the only contagion on PrEP that ever happened, one case in many millions, and it seems it was provoked by a series of uneventful consequences, so there's no real risk for anyone. And the other STDs didn't bother me anymore, since no one is life-threatening.

The tests I usually do are for HIV, Hepatitis C, syphilis, gonorrhea and chlamydia. They're fast and you get the results by SMS a few hours later.

I was there on Thursday after a few months. They took me a drop of blood for HIV and syphilis, another one for Hepatitis C, and I needed to put those cotton buds inside my throat, the arse and, the most painful, urethra.

A few hours later, as always, I got four SMS messages.

TDL: Your Hepatitis C test was negative (clear)

TDL: Your syphilis test was negative (clear). You do not need any treatment.

TDL: Your HIV test was negative (clear)

DSE: Hello. Your non-blood test(s) for Chlamydia was negative (clear). Anything caught within the last 2 weeks may not be detected. Here's a summary:
Chlamydia
Rectal: Negative
Throat: Negative
Urine: Negative

I didn't even notice that in the last message I didn't get the results for gonorrhea.

It was on Friday morning when I got a call. It was from the testing center. They told me there was nothing to worry about, but I needed to show up there.

I went there on Friday after work and the doctor told me I had gonorrhea. Although I've read in some newspaper that the OMS put gonorrhea on the list of untreatable diseases, this is only because in some countries it has become resistant to all types of known antibiotics. But this was not the case in the UK, for the moment. With two pills of azithromycin it would have disappeared in less than ten days. Meanwhile, I should not have any sexual contact for two weeks.

EUSTON, WE HAVE A PROBLEM

I just got it diagnosed a few hours before the party at my place was going to start. Would I have to cancel the event? Absolutely not. I needed company, I needed my "friends", I needed someone to touch me and to feel human touch.

I also had no visible symptoms, so I could just start taking antibiotics on Monday.

If I stopped the party, what the hell would I have done for the whole weekend? I'd have died of boredom.

And here's my ass, full of sperm, that has now lost its initial warmth but is still inside me. Surrounded by people that are fucking with each other, not ever noticing how fucked up I am.

I can't move any of my muscles. And I know nobody's going to help me. I just want everyone to leave.

Many people say they would like to die while fucking. I don't think it's a fantasy, it's just considered a good way to end your life. And I have the sensation that I'm about to die, just after being fucked.

It's funny, as a child in the province, I was always watching TV, seeing that glittering world that was so far away from our rural reality, and I wanted to be part of it. I was hoping that one day I'll have the opportunity to be on that shiny TV screen. It never happened, but if I die that way, there's a possibility that my photo will be in The Daily Mirror in the following days.

People are fucking careless around me, and I can just see a vinyl on my wall. We bought it with Matthias in a cheap Chinese shop. "Life is not measured by the number of breaths we take, but by the moments that take our breath away". I was breathless, living life, or thinking I was doing so.

ADAM KACZINSKY

What would Matthias think about me if he saw me now?

His best friend, on drugs, fucked by his boyfriend, dying of an overdose.

10 FUCKING HERE AND THERE

People judge chemsex parties, saying they are not normal. But let's be sincere. What is normal? I am maybe not the best one to answer this question, since all my life I've been different.

At school, I didn't like football. And this was not normal since all the boys loved football. I was the only left-handed student in the class, again not normal. And in small environments differences are never considered a gift, they're the topic of all gossiping instead. So when I discovered I was gay I didn't feel like sharing it with anybody.

Interesting fact, many people knew I was gay much before I found it out, but none of them were local. I was about 15 when aunt Alessandra, who was living in Rome and was not my aunt but the aunt of a school friend of mine, but I don't know why, all of us in the village were calling her aunt, told me that being gay was normal, and that she had a lot of gay friends who were living a really normal life there in the Italian capital. It happened when some of my school friends were imitating some of my walking moves, which were probably not so masculine.

First of all, why did she tell me that? She was supposing I was gay, but I was not. I liked girls, because this was normal, although I've still never been with one of them. And how could aunt Alessandra say that gay people live a normal life if we all know that gays are not normal?

At that point I didn't even think I could be gay, I was straight, straight, straight! Gays didn't exist in my town in Poland. I just started to hate aunt Alessandra because she suggested that this could be an option for me.

I discovered that I was gay only one or two years later, during our beach holidays with my cousin Agata. Her older brother was employed for the season in the town of Hel, in the northern region, and he could host us for a week in a camping tent in front of his apartment. I was a minor and Agata was two years younger than me, so her brother was supposed to take care of us when he was not working. On the second day of our holiday, while walking on the sandy beach, I found out that my eyes were not looking at what's hidden behind the female bikinis. My look was fixed on the male slips and boxers, wondering how it looked that thing behind them.

This was just not possible. I couldn't be gay. I was out of myself for the rest of the day. Back in the tent, in the evening, I was just not able to interact with Agata. I used the first pretext to have the biggest fight ever with her. I obviously don't remember the reason, because there was no reason, and I remember even less the arguments I used. But the following morning we took a bus back to our town, four days before it was planned, we were finishing our holidays. I felt the anger. Anger against myself for being attracted to males. And I used this anger to attack Agata, because she was there at the moment. Whoever would have been at her place when I discovered to be gay would have been the victim of my anger.

EUSTON, WE HAVE A PROBLEM

When we came back to my hometown, my mind had somehow forgotten about the male organs I've been trying to identify through the speedos of the bathers. Just months later, hidden in my room, I've discovered that there were online chats for gays.

Pawel was the first person I met online, my first love and my first kiss. Olek my first cum in the ass.

I went to university, aware of being gay, but didn't come out to anyone. And didn't even try to get to know someone. During the last year at the university, I met Mikolaj, a student of architecture that was living life and did not have time to finish his studies for about a decade. He was born in my hometown and well educated, so I've found a friend to share my doubts. Mikolaj was just this, nothing more. Actually, this was meaning a lot for me. I was full of questions that may have sounded stupid, but for Mikolaj they weren't. He has lived an experience similar to mine, so he was happy to help.

It was at the time when low-cost airlines were starting to fly people for cheap prices. Mikolaj found a cheap ticket to Barcelona, and this was my first trip ever out of Poland, as well as my first random sex.

As an enthusiast but never graduated architect, Mikolaj was planning all the sightseeing, and he let me take care of the nightlife. Gay, obviously. I remember running up and down the large avenues of the Catalan city, Mikolaj taking me inside the Casa Battló, La Pedrera, La Sagrada Familia and then walking for kilometers to see a photovoltaic at the Fórum, almost at the edge of the city. But what I most remember is seeing gays on the street. Some of them were even holding their hands. All this was almost unbelievable.

The night was even more exciting. There was a whole neighborhood near the University square dedicated to gay people, called Eixample Izquierdo. The first bar we visited was called Átame, as the original title of the movie "Tie Me Up! Tie me down" of Pedro Almodóvar. The bar was actually pretty empty, with Eurovision-style pop music, a video wall and a pool table. After a gin tonic, we moved to the bar next door, named Dietrich. This one was nicer, fuller and with a small tropical garden at the end, and a live show that was just starting. There was the first time I've seen drag queens performing, but also a black muscled man dancing in thongs on cloth curtains. The last drink we had was at Zéltas, a few blocks away, and I can remember that, for being a bar, some people were even too explicit. Many of the guests were south-Americans, when we were leaving Mikolaj told me that several of them were looking like prostitutes.

Mikolaj had a strong fever so he went back to the hostel. I was feeling drunk and left for a disco called Arena Madre. There, looking for a bathroom in the basement, I've ended up in the dark room. At that point, I still didn't differentiate sex from love, and the images I saw of people sucking each other were too shocking for me. I didn't want to stay there anymore, so I've left for another disco I had on my list: Metro. Since I was in Barcelona, I wanted to see it all in one night. Metro was on the way back home. I still remember waiting in the queue, then going down the stairs, the place full of smoke. At that time, smoking was still allowed everywhere.

There were two music rooms and a bar in the middle. The smaller room, with pop music, but at least a hundred gays there. Oh my god, I've never seen a hundred gays. And they all danced and looked happy. I went for my last gin tonic and moved to the other room which, surprisingly, was enormous. The music was techno, with green lasers moving through the hall and at least a thousand people. It was like all the gays of the world were in Barcelona right now. I hated techno, but as I was entering the room, I saw him, a good-looking muscular guy dancing and looking directly at me from the middle of the dance floor.

I went straightforward to him. I tried to dance but was not able either. We shared my gin and tonic, and I kissed him. He touched my cock, which got hard immediately, and we left. I didn't speak Spanish, he didn't speak Polish, and we both almost didn't know a word of English, but we were walking together through Barcelona, kissing on the street on our way to my hostel. I kicked out Mikolaj from our room, and he waited for a few hours on the street for us to finish. It was my first night of sex only, the first time I had sex for sex, without involving emotions. But there still was some human side that today I'm missing.

His name was Jordi and he invited Mikolaj and me to a party at a friend's home the next day. During I day I slept, while Mikolaj was visiting Montjüic, the Olympic hill and some arts and architecture foundations. When we arrived to the house where the party was held, I've found out Jordi was ugly as sin. The lights at the disco and the gin and tonic made him look so awesome the night before.

After Jordi, I didn't have sex for sex for a long while.

During my Erasmus period in Italy, at the University of Bologna, I met a boy through a gay website. His name was Emanuele and we were meeting at a square two evenings a week, sitting on a bench, me again asking a lot of questions, he giving me some decent answers. It was like some kind of relationship, but the most we did together was kissing and hugging on a public square. Maybe it would have gone further, but he was living with his mother and grandmother, and I was too poor to go out with his friends at the time. Emanuele cared about me. Fifteen years later, he is still writing to me at least once every few weeks to check how my life is going.

It was at a dinner with school colleagues during the Erasmus exchange I've met Michele. We stayed in contact after that dinner and when I told him I was looking for a partner for conversations to improve my Italian, he offered himself. We were meeting a few evenings a week at a bar on Pratello Street, getting to know each other speaking in a language that was not mine. It was a challenge for me, and also very exciting. There was no given topic, it was just conversations, so we were talking about the arts, history, economics, life, love, and sex, depending on our mood. Michele was openly gay, and speaking with him has become more and more interesting. Our meetings lasted as long as we didn't finish the bottle of sparkling Pignoletto local wine he loved. And the end of any of our conversations was starting to convert more and more into flirting. Each time I was having a meeting scheduled with Michele, I was excited from the morning, waiting to see him.

It all started with a kiss at the bar, helped by the wine. One of the next times, he invited me to have our meeting at his place, and I stayed there to sleep. Through the months, we were having wild sex on his sofa bed, and I slept in his attic more than at my student residence. So he thought it was a good idea to give me a copy of his keys.

I was feeling insecure about Michele because during our conversation meetings in Italian he had told me about a lot of sexual experiences, and I couldn't trust that he only stayed with me. To assure myself he will not be unfaithful, I was giving him all of my sexual energy and sometimes I felt he wanted more and wilder.

I was preparing for my finals exams in Italy, and on a Friday night he asked me to join him for the weekend. I told him it was impossible, I had much left to study, and he was ok with it. He would stay home and watching movies all weekend.

EUSTON, WE HAVE A PROBLEM

On Saturday, around midnight, I decided I've studied enough, and my brain was not absorbing anything more anyway. So I called him. But his mobile phone was off. I still remember walking through the center of Bologna and reaching his apartment. He was supposed to watch movies and I wanted surprise him, he would love it. But when I opened the door, the surprise was all for me: there were two pairs of shoes, two pairs of pants and two sweaters on the floor, as well as moans coming from his room. I've left the keys inside and left, and never wanted to speak to Michele again. But I also felt guilty that I refused to meet him, as well as guilty of not giving him enough sex.

My self-esteem was below zero. And it was only the beginning of a long series of stories with the same pattern.

My first love story in London, if we can call it that, was not much better. Amanda, a colleague from work who wanted to be a matchmaker, was trying to convince me to meet a friend of hers that was the ideal man for me, according to her. I refused because I didn't want love to be something planned, especially by people who think if they have a gay friend, it will match with a gay colleague they have, only because they're both gay.

But Amanda didn't give up. She knew the exact time I was leaving the office, and one Monday afternoon she was down with him, waiting for me. They both acted as they've casually met, and invited me to a beer. I didn't have anything planned, so I joined them, for a beer only. The truth is that he was interesting and cute. The only thing I didn't like about him, he was out of town for work four days a week. I don't know how, after many beers, we all ended up at my place. He started to roll a joint, and Amanda said she was tired and needed to go home since she was working in the morning. I was working in the morning too, but he was not willing to leave. When he finished his joint, I started to yawn. He told me he was dizzy from the joint, so I offered him to sleep at my place. We made love at some point during the night.

In the morning we had a coffee in the kitchen and he told me he'd like to see me again. I told him it was a pleasure, but I was not considering at all to start something serious with someone that's away for work for more than half of each week, travelling through all the UK. I knew I would not be able to. "Like sailors, I'm sure you have a lover in every port", I told him.

I would never leave someone alone at my place, less if it was a hookup stranger. But I was late to go to work, he was nice and he was a friend of Amanda. So I told him he could take a shower and get dressed without stress. When I came back home, I found a handwritten poem on my bed. He was serious in trying to conquer me.

When I saw the poem, he was already on a flight to Edinburgh. I got a lot of messages from him during that week, as well as emails with photos from his hotel and the dinners he was having alone.

He came back on Friday evening, showing up at my door with a bouquet of red roses. I always thought that flowers were a female thing, but he wanted to show me that he cared and this was nice.

We've been together for two years. He's always been out of town Tuesday to Friday, the weekends intensely together. During that period I could never lower my guard, I couldn't trust him totally.

I knew that, before he met me, Edward had fallen in love with Julien, a Canadian guy who was in a relationship with a powerful businessman who was out of the city most of the time. Edward would have started a serious relationship with him, but Julien was not interested in breaking his relationship. So they were just fucking together when Julien's boyfriend was away. They supposedly stopped seeing each other when Edward met me.

During the first year Edward proposed to invite Julien for a dinner or a theatre show with us, I thought this was not ok at all, they have been lovers before and I didn't see why he should join us. I have to say that Edward didn't insist.

It was December 19th and Edward was working in London the whole week. Since he was not located far from my office, we would meet to pass my lunch break together. At the last minute he called me, saying he had an unplanned meeting with a customer and he couldn't join, so I could stay in Canary Wharf. I had planned to have good food, so despite Edward's cancellation I took the tube and went to his favorite restaurant. But when I entered, there was him, sitting at a table and having lunch with Julien.

At the time there was still no WhatsApp. I've sent him a few insults by SMS, went back to work and didn't reply to his phone calls later. He wrote me an email, saying that Julien was going to Canada the following day with his boyfriend, and he wanted to wish him a merry Christmas. He didn't want me to know about it, because I wouldn't approve it. Again, I felt paranoid, mistrustful and guilty.

But I was right. It was just after Christmas, a cold Sunday afternoon. After we watched a movie, I still did not feel good for all that had passed with Julien, I went to clean the flat and he used my computer to do some work. When he left, I went to my laptop to call my mother on Skype, but there was a surprise. The web browser was opened and logged into an email address that was not his, or at least not the official one I knew. I was about to close it when I saw one of the subjects was "Orgy Cardiff". I opened about twenty emails one by one, they were full of information about meetings, locations, and sexual preferences, sent and received during the two years we have been together. This was also a catalog of photos of the people he met. In the "Sent messages" folder I could find photos of his cock, his ass, sometimes also his face.

How can one feel when he discovers that or two years he has been living in lies? Now I knew it. I knew that he was buying me roses and writing me poems at the same time that he was opening his ass to strangers during his travels around the UK.

I also knew my suspects were not unfounded from the beginnings. I should have trusted my sixth sense, I should trust it from now on. But my sixth sense has become too sensitive, always on alert. And since in almost all my relationships happened the same, I didn't know if I'll ever be able to lower the guard.

Before Edward, I had more experiences of people lying to me in the same way. But this time it lasted for two years. Two lost years in my life, sharing my bed, my intimacy with someone that was always fucking around. So I came to the conclusion that all men are the same: they all want to have both romance and freedom for one night stands at the same time. They want to feel intimate, make life plans with someone, but out there there's so much new to discover, and they don't want to be deprived of it. To fulfill both needs at the same time, the only solution is lying. And I was one of the victims of such behavior.

My friend Matthias was thinking this is something more connected to karma, and to the law of attraction. We were both always attracting the same kind of person, selling us the world and wanting just a fuck.

After Edward, I met a few people who were offering something too good to be true. I started to feel that the gay world is based on marketing: you need to sell yourself the best you can, you need to enter the brain of another person and offer them exactly what they're looking for. That's the only way you get to shag with them.

There's one sexual practice I found honest: open-air cruising. I was on holidays alone on a beach in Costa Brava called Sant Pol de Mar. South of town, there's a nudist beach made of many small bays of heavy golden sand. I was lying alone in one of them reading a book when a gorgeous boy appeared with a hard cock. It took me a few seconds and I got hard too. He sucked me for a good fifteen minutes. When I jerked off, he told me it was great. He also told me he saw me from a rock, but had to wait a good while to get hard and come down to the bay because I was the fourth one he was with today. It can feel disgusting knowing that your cock had just been in a mouth that sucked other three cocks in the previous few hours, but it was not. That guy was honest.

At a cruising people normally don't go around telling you how many cocks they have sucked before getting into yours, but nobody also lies that he is there only for you and that is offering you love. There you know what you can find and know what you get. Isn't that fair?

When I felt horny, I had a walk to Hampstead Heath, Hyde Park or Clapham Common at night and if I found someone I liked, we relieved each other's stress in between the trees. Although, it is more fun to cruise where the climate is warmer and it's more pleasant to be naked.

Through the years I've discovered that any place is potentially a cruising spot, and I sharpened my sight in finding cruising places. Although one of the biggest cruisings in the world is the Dunes of Gran Canaria, I didn't like it. There I've always found a lot of desperate, old, kinky tourists, and although there was a load of possibilities, I've never found anyone decent there to have sex with.

Until I found out that only a mile away there was a night cruising area only for locals, just near a roundabout facing the camel safari. I've left my soul in that sand, and a lot of cum too. During one of my many travels to Barcelona, I went to Montjüic, a big hill not far from the center and one of the biggest open-air dark rooms of the world at night, open 365 days a year.

When cruising, I normally prefer an one-to-one meeting and leave. But there I've just lost control. After walking through the paths for a while, I met a hot young boy and we went inside the woods. I knelt down and started to suck him. Shortly afterwards, a second bloke appeared, even cuter, more hung and harder. On my knees, I was switching from one cock to another. When the first one was up to jerk off, a couple of muscular guys entered the woods from the path. I was on my knees and everyone wanted my mouth. I felt pain in the ligaments, but felt powerful choosing whose turn it was next. I've been there for at least an hour, sucking about ten people, all of them coming out of my dreams, or at least from a fashion catalog. I have not rejected any of them. Some of them wanted to fuck me, but I was never doing this outdoors, and less with strangers.

On my way back through the path, a masculine young boy was running in his white stretch shorts showing there was a lot there behind. I sat on a bench and took off my pants, leaving them on the bench. He stopped, looking at me. I was wearing running shoes and rugby socks which almost reached my knees. I opened my legs, put each foot on one side of the bench and started to masturbate. He approached the bench, knelt down in front of me and started to give me pleasure with his tongue. I was enjoying the blowjob, touching his nipples and looking at his defined hairy legs. While he was sucking me, a few guys passed, me showing them with my face to go away. He was sucking in and out my balls one after the other. I opened my legs even more and with his tongue, he went right inside my ass hole. As he was doing circles with his wet tongue, I jerked off moaning noisily. At that same moment, a voice shouted: "Stop, police". On our right side, there were two uniformed policemen. I took my pants and ran away half-naked as fast as I could. Just after a few minutes of running through the park with my cock outside, I went inside the woods and dressed again. I could have been arrested for obscene acts in public. But that night was fun.

I came back again the following night. I walked around the same park for about four or five hours. Although there were a lot of people, this time there was none of my taste. This actually happens frequently on cruising, if one has a minimum of criteria. I'll remember that first night at Montjüic as something special, unlikely to happen ever again.

When I arrived in London, I was sharing a flat with a Greek boy. One Friday evening, a colleague from work invited me to have a pizza, but I refused. I went home to read a book I wanted to finish. Around nine, I started to feel stupid. I started to think that at this time of the weekend everyone else in London was partying, getting drunk and having fun, while I was in my bed staring at a book, at the beginning of my Thirties. I opened Grindr, starting to look for sex now, just not feeling different from the rest of the world. But for the following two hours I didn't find anyone who could host me. Since I was unable to arrange a fuck date, I decided to go down to Hyde Park, promising myself I'll suck the first one I meet. The issue is I had some criteria and the first one I met was not only older than Satan, but looking really disgusting, so I waited for the following one. The second one was not better at all, and so the third. I passed the night smoking cigarettes and walking through Hyde Park. It was around five in the morning when I noticed someone that could be acceptable. Acceptable, but not so much for letting his cock inside my mouth. We wanked together, and after a fast jerk off I went back home to sleep. When I woke up it was almost afternoon, my flatmate asked me how the night had been. I told him the story and I remember my last sentence. "It would have been much better if I had gone to the pizza place, and then jerked off alone in my bed". Because, even if I find cruising as an honest compromise where nobody lies to you, I know it's just a distraction. In the end, I don't get what I really need.

Sexual addiction is another frequent reason why people lie.

I met Philippe on a long train ride from Glasgow to home. He was sitting in front of me and, with an excuse, he started to talk to me at the beginning of the journey. The train was pretty empty and the 4 and a half hours of the ride passed extremely quickly, switching from topic to topic. He had an interesting life story. He moved to the UK after the restaurant he was running with his boyfriend in Paris was burnt, which was also the cause of the break-up. Now he was doing an office job, working night shifts, one week on, another off, which meant he was free half of the month. In his free time, he was doing voluntary work for an organization to prevent HIV infections.

When we arrived at Euston station, he asked me if I wanted to have a drink. I told him I was living two minutes away, and we could have it at my place. About five minutes after entering the flat, I was fucking with him. About an hour later, my cock was inside him again: after the fuck, we had a shower, and while we've been drinking that drink, his head descended at the height of my soft cock, his tongue making it hard again, so I began to fuck him for the third time.

That night he slept with me and I didn't even unpack the suitcase I brought from Glasgow. In the morning, we fucked twice before I went to work.

In the following months, I started to see Philippe regularly. When he was not working, we were passing the week intensively together, doing many things, but most of them being sex. I couldn't tell anyone of us felt love, but he was the only person I had seen for many months, we were having our toothbrushes in each other's flat. This was for me a symbol of monogamy.

I also started to introduce Philippe to my friends. At the summer party of my company he met my work colleagues and, at a Sunday hipster food market, I've met some friends of him from the HIV prevention association. I already knew one of them, he was the one that was taking care of my HIV and syphilis tests for a few years. That night we fucked bareback. We did it five times before sleeping, one more time when we woke up. He was going to start the full night shift week, so we used our last night at full, leaving me without a drop.

During the lunch break, my colleague Olivia, who was living in Vauxhall, told me that in the morning, on her way to work, she saw that French friend of mine entering the biggest European gay sauna. There must have been a mistake, I thought. We passed most of our time together, and most of our time together was sex.

Back on the phone with my customers, I was tense, my body temperature became higher and my mouth dry. I couldn't listen to them. I was seeing images of me fucking him raw, then he being fucked by strangers in the sauna.

I was up to finish my shift when I decided to download Hornet. It was an app like Grindr, but you could search for people by location. I created a profile quickly, just to check if he'd be there. Since I was not planning to find him, I didn't even bother to put my age or to find a photo for my profile.

It was 4:45 in the afternoon, my customer explaining me his problem over the phone when I pinned the map over Fortress Road, Tufnell

Park and started the search. And guess who was online? Philippe, showing his actual face pic. I offered him sex now in my hotel, saying I was top only. He replied, asking which hotel. My customer was still explaining his story, I was not listening at all. I opened Google Maps and looked for hotels near his home. There was no hotel around, and the closest one was the Premier Inn in Archway. I wrote to him that I was there and very horny, again, looking for now. His reply was not a text, just a series of photos of his ass from all angles, and a dick pic.

All the men wanted to have a relationship and free fucks at the same time, and they needed to lie to be able to get both. I should have already learned that. But there was more: how is it possible that, after fucking six times in one night, someone feels the need to go to a sauna for a full morning, and in the afternoon, before going to work, needs more sex? I don't have any other explanation than calling it an addiction. And a strong one.

Since I didn't want to believe what I've just heard and seen, I wanted to check again. I did a second profile that same night, when he was working. Sending him a random cock photo I've found on the internet, I've invited him to join me at the hotel where I supposedly was staying, just three minutes away from his office. He replied to me that he was working right now, but if I was available a bit later, he was having a break at 3 AM.

A month later I went to the HIV prevention association to get tested. The doctor, the one I had met at the hipster food truck exactly a month before, asked me how life with Philippe was. I just replied that we were not together, not entering into details.

In this association, I was always offered to test for HIV and syphilis only. At that time the doctor told me they had some new tests: a blood test for HIV that detects the antigen P24, which is much more likely to find recently acquired HIV than standard test, but there were also some new tests, for hepatitis C, chlamydia and gonorrhea. I had never been offered these tests before, so I suspected it could be connected to the doctor seeing me with Philippe. The condition to get tested was to sign a document stating that I was a prostitute, or had sex with at least 60 people in the last 180 days. I was not fulfilling any of the requirements, but the doctor insisted on me signing it. That was the way the national health system was going to cover the cost of the tests. End of the story is I was lucky, I only got positive for chlamydia, in the throat, ass, and cock, but I could get rid of it with only one pill.

11 HOW IT ALL STARTED

So how could a conservative boy, paranoid with all the STDs become the king of London's party and play? I have no clue.

There have probably been a series of factors that led me unconsciously here.

The first time I ever used drugs was with two colleagues. Gergely and Abraham, from Hungary and Spain respectively, invited me to join them in a club. After a few minutes of dancing, they invited me to join them in the toilet. There they offered me something I've never heard about before, called MDMA. I was scared, didn't want to try any drugs, but I also wanted to feel like I have friends in the city, I didn't want to be an outsider. So I tried it. And again, and again, for hours. At some point, Gergely and Abraham lost me.

They found me in another hall, putting my tongue inside the mouth of any boy and girl that was on my way. It was a club for straight people, but no one was complaining, no one refused my kisses. My colleagues told me I was in a really bad condition, and they would have taken me home. Waiting for the cab, I started to touch

Gergely's belly. I still remember how I could feel his soft skin and, under it, the muscles under his abs. It was not a sexual activity, but I loved it. Gergely was straight, and we never spoke about that night ever. But I decided drugs are not for me. I just needed to learn how to kindly refuse such invitations if I got one again.

The first time I took drugs for having sex, it was at one of my first hookups ever in London. I got it offered and again didn't know to say no. A Colombian guy named Pablo invited me to fuck at his place in Peckham. He was a young but already respected contemporary art critic. When I arrived there, he was still writing a review that he needed to submit to be published in a catalog. On the table, there were several lines of coke. He apologized, he had a deadline and he was writing as fast as possible. As soon as he's done, we'll fuck as agreed. He was really fast, writing a complicated arts review while having a deep, interesting conversation with me at the same time. His text had no typos and the things he was asking me were really interesting. I felt he was present in both activities. He even took a phone call, meanwhile, looking like a perfect multi-tasker. He really believed in himself, giving value to what he was doing. His ego was something I always wanted and didn't have.

During that half an hour, he offered me coke a few times. I initially refused, but then I tried it, just not to be a party breaker. When it came to sex, he was sniffing all night. It was a long session, hours of fucking it, my cock already hurting and not being able to jerk off. I wanted it all to be finished, but the end was not near. At some point, while fucking him, I became aggressive. I started to shout at him, gave him a punch, got dressed and left.

We have been using condoms during the whole act. What really turned me off, he was using a rubber cock ring to stay hard. This made me feel like I was not turning him on enough. I have always been insecure, and the only time I tried coke I got aggressive because of that.

I decided not to try cocaine again.

I tried crystal meth with a guy I met on Grindr and I started hooking up regularly with Francesco. He was Italian and he was having an open relationship with a British bloke. They had an agreement: every Saturday night they could enjoy other's bodies separately. It was a decision of the two, so I didn't mind. Actually, his boyfriend was normally taking him to my place.

It was the first time I was meeting someone that was in an open couple, or at least the first time I was told that. But I found their relationship to be honest and transparent, so I didn't mind meeting with Francesco. Our sex meetings were not a fuck-and-go thing. We had dinner, wine, music and preliminaries. And it used to last for the whole night. He never slept at my place, though. He was taking the train back to his boyfriend's home on Sunday in the early morning.

Our meetings became frequent. We were meeting with each other for two Saturdays a month. It was almost like some relationship. Not a real one, since he already had a boyfriend, but it was nice to repeat with the same person, getting to know each other's bodies and knowing what each other liked. I always supposed that his Saturday sex outside of home was something that was keeping his relationship alive. From my experience, monogamous relationships in the gay world doesn't exist. And he found a good compromise. I also admired the transparency he and his boyfriend had in handling their lives. Although they were fucking around with other people, they could still have mutual trust.

EUSTON, WE HAVE A PROBLEM

When it came to penetration, I was always fucking Francesco and never the way around. But he always wanted to fuck me. He knew that I couldn't, that for me it would have been too painful, probably because of psychological reasons, but my ass was not letting anybody in.

One Saturday, sitting on my sofa, he took something like a sweets wrapper out of his bag. He opened it and inside there was some white powder. He asked me to lick it all together, saying it was crystal and was making sex much more enjoyable. Half an hour later I was on my bed, staying on all fours, he was riding me. I lied down, turned around, my back and shoulders on the bed, legs up, he entered inside and outside me, feeling a sensation of heat through all the body, like burning of pleasure. I was in another dimension, having a sense of satisfaction I've never had before.

He was fucking me raw, I was aware of it. I enjoyed it so much and was unable to stop it. I actually didn't want him to stop. We both jerked off at the same time, over my stomach. Luckily, he didn't do it inside.

But he was having a boyfriend, they were having regular sex, and the boyfriend was meeting other people too, so fucking raw with him was exponentially dangerous.

Again, as with coke and MDMA, I promised myself I'll never try that again.

After the effect of crystal meth ended, I became anxious. The anxiety lasted for three full months, until I got tested. At that time I was lucky. I didn't get anything. I've actually always been lucky, apart from the chlamydia I've got from Philippe.

In the last few years, I've started to hear about PrEP. It was a medication that, if taken every day, was preventing you from being infected by HIV. The main reason it was put on the market were couples where one of the partners was HIV positive, and the other not. If the HIV-negative partner was regularly taking PrEP, the couple could have a better sexual life, no need for a condom, and the negative partner not getting infected. Having said this, PrEP is helpful for anyone, since it is very effective.

Although PrEP was expensive, there were a lot of people that started to use it for another reason: having condomless sex with whoever, which was also exponentially spreading the possibility for everyone to get some other STDs. As a real hypochondriac, I was disgusted by that idea.

I never liked condoms. They were marking a distance, disrupting any possible feeling of intimacy, but they were also fundamental to protecting ourselves in a world full of STDs. I was not as paranoid as Matthias, but taking precautions was really necessary.

During my holidays in Thailand, in a pharmacy in Bangkok's Silom quarter, I've found some pills they've been advertising as PrEP. They were fucking cheap. They were not Truvada, which was supposed to be the only original PrEP. They were called Teno-Em, and the pharmacist told me they were exactly the same as Truvada. I bought a few boxes as a joke, the price was ridiculously low, and I didn't have any aim of using them ever.

Back in London, after Mattias died, I spoke to my doctor, and he confirmed that Teno-Em was a combination of Tenofovir and Emtricitabine, the two drugs that constitute Truvada, and its effects would not differ from the "original" product. Again, I didn't plan to use them.

But I was weak and vulnerable, I was feeling completely lost and I was not able to interact with anyone. The painting I was doing at the time was getting darker and darker. I was not able to recover from the loss of Matthias.

When I wanted human touch, I started to speak through Grindr with people, feeling even worse. All was so inhuman, I didn't want to meet anyone. My idea that I'll never find someone in London that can be faithful and so I'll never have a normal relationship made me desperate. I needed to feel some human touch, I needed a hug, but I knew something like this was not on offer, anywhere. And I got scared of the idea of getting touched by any random people from Grindr.

I was not pertaining to any group. I was not a hipster, neither an emo nor a cub, I was just me. And I was alone, with no perspective. I had no possibility to satisfy my basic needs. I was feeling cold inside, and nobody was there to warm my soul up.

One morning, after I woke up and had breakfast, almost as a joke, I swallowed a pill of Teno-Em. The following morning I did it again. And the next one again, and so on.

For a few months, I was taking PrEP without even touching anyone. Then, I found the courage to meet a boy from Grindr. When I arrived at his place, I wanted to go back. I was not feeling ready to touch anyone. But I was already there, so I couldn't cancel a meeting again. I didn't show up at so many hookups in the last months, this time I needed to be brave and do it.

Once in there, I didn't feel comfortable at all. He could feel my stress even at a distance. I was getting undressed and feeling shy. He started to touch me, but I was so tense. It is at that point that he offered to try something. It was the crystal meth I already knew, but there was another substance, meph, I've never tried before.

And I said to myself why not. I needed to relax and enjoy it. So after a few hours of wild sweaty sex and deep pleasure, we took GHB too. We've been alone at his place for a day and a half, and I was wild, not shy at all.

When I came back home I couldn't remember if we ever used a condom during that weekend. But I felt relieved. I was taking PrEP. There was no risk. It is interesting how my brain decided only to focus on the HIV the PrEP was protecting me, and has completely erased any idea about the possibility of getting any other STD.

I became more sexually liberated. PrEP took away all my fears. With PrEP I was feeling comfortable and safe.

I've lived all my life with the fear of getting infected. And I remembered the same fear that drove Matthias to take his life. I didn't want to end the same way as him. And that day, thanks to PrEP, I've completely lost that fear I was having during all these years. Realizing that, my mindset changed in half a second.

Then, I changed my Grindr status to "Negative - on prep" and started to get contacted by more and more people. I wanted to repeat experiences such as the one I've just lived in, so I started to meet only guys doing chems. Sometimes it was one-to-one, other times it was a *party'n'play*. And I discovered as many more people there are, many more you have. Chemsex became a regular part of my life, first once a month, then every two weeks, and now it's every weekend.

And the shy, introverted boy that was in me has disappeared.

EUSTON, WE HAVE A PROBLEM

I was always surrounded by good-looking strangers, all of them interested in me. I was living a dream. It was an exciting sensation. Being the center of attention made me feel powerful and euphoric. And I was finally getting the physical contact I always needed. And I had the possibility to have this every weekend.

I was feeling that my social life has definitely improved. And my biggest fantasy had been fulfilled: when I watched porn, it was usually bareback orgies, gangbangs. Before PrEP I'd never had any of these two, but now I was living the porn movie myself.

There's a small invisible line there in between being a sporadic user experimenting with drugs and the moment when you need these drugs to go on. With MDMA and coke, I could stop. With the party'n'play chems, I became addicted from the beginning.

Immediately after I started with chems, I had one Grindr hookup without taking any. I felt uncomfortable, I could not relax, could not get horny. I was totally unable to enjoy sex unless chems.

And in the last half of the year, I haven't had sex sober one only at a time.

But addiction was not only for chems.

I also needed sex. I was living for next Friday. And I always needed more.

I'm now lying down alone on the bed, completely unconscious, and I can see myself from above, like an image recorded by a drone.

Through my mind, I see the faces of the people I've hooked up to in the last year. I've had more than 700 sexual partners. If I tell this to some straight friend of mine, they would never be able to believe this. My mind is showing me images of each one of them. With most of them I exchanged fluids. During that period I also got seven kisses, one of them actually only to exchange some third guy's sperm. And I got no hug at all.

The last time I got a hug, it was with Diego.

12. DIEGO

After all my experiences, I couldn't trust anyone. I was having anonymous sex while cruising, once every few months, when I desperately needed the human touch. And that was all. If I found somebody I could match with and that could be similar to me I was fast in finding an excuse why this would not work, and so it was not even worth trying it. I didn't want to get hurt anymore and I kept myself distant from anyone.

I adopted borderline behavior for people not having even the temptation to get close to me, to want to know get to know anything more about me. And the price of this behavior has been paid by Diego.

I met Diego in a bookshop at St. Pancras station. I've been living in London for ten years, and when the Brexit negotiations started, I didn't know what was going to happen to my UK residence card when the UK left the EU, so I decided to take the test "Life in the UK", which was one of the conditions for requesting British citizenship. To pass the exam, there was a book with all the possible questions at the test.

At the bookshop in St. Pancras, Diego was buying the same book as me. He was Spanish and was facing the same issues and doubts about residing in the UK as was I. In the bookshop, we started to talk about how stupid all this Brexit shit was and we ended up having coffee. We were both agreeing that Brexit was a wrong choice. Not only was it affecting us, putting us in an unknown status, British people would lose a lot too. Diego told me this was something like when Geri Halliwell overestimated her viability as a solo artist and left the Spice Girls.

We decided we could study for the exam together. We met twice a week, revising potential questions for the test. At the beginning it was at a bar in Kentish Town, then it was my place or at his. Twice a week, for a few hours, we were studying the life of the royal family, the colours of the Welsh flag, the fundamental principles of British life, the traditional foods of each of the countries, the overseas territories, the Commonwealth, the roles of the House of Commons, the House of Lords, as well as the ones of the Monarch and the Prime Minister. We also reviewed all the music festivals on the island and came to know how many years have passed the Romans in the UK. Long story short, nothing romantic.

One evening he asked me to stay for dinner and to watch a football match with him, he loved football. He was cooking salmon and there was enough for two. I didn't love football, but I accepted it, with one condition. During dinner, we should not speak about Anne Boleyn, Henry Purcell, the Bill of Rights, the Swinging Sixties or anything related to the Scottish Parliament. So while he was cooking, I went down and bought a bottle of white wine.

That night we started to speak about each other's dreams and plans for the future, to get to know each other better. Before he came to London, Diego had a girlfriend for many years. He managed to partially accept his homosexuality only on the anonymity of the big city, but in ten years of living here he didn't get too much experience in the field: what was on offer was too heavy for him.

We both thought London was not a good place to get old. Too big, too lonely. We were both seeing each other getting retired in a warmer, sunnier and quieter place by the beach, with a dog, maybe even two children. I've suggested that his home country Spain could be a good option, perhaps the Malaga region. At that point, he googled a town called Nerja, and the photos he showed me were as the place I've always dreamed about. His brother was living there, and Diego was totally committed to his family. Every few weeks he was flying either to Barcelona, to pass time with his mother, or to Malaga, to stay with his brother's children. Before flying to Malaga he used to rehearse magic tricks, as his nephews were convinced their uncle was a magician.

But we both agreed retirement was not nearly so close. There were still a lot of things to do before. One of them, recurring the whole world, was trying to get ourselves a job as freelancers. Not to make money, just to survive while exploring the world and living new experiences. He told me if we wanted to do it, he just needed to give 30 days notice before leaving his job. I got excited, started to think about how good it would be to share a trip with a friend like him, and wondered what kind of job we could do to survive. We didn't even kiss that night, we did much more: before I left, he pulled me into his big arms, stretched into a long, strong hug. Through the pullover, I felt his skin was burning, I felt the human warmth I was missing so much in London and I felt safe and protected. I didn't need sex to be happy. I needed illusion, protection and shared life plans for all my problems to disappear.

Not all, actually. Some of them just arose after I met Diego.

During a ride in the bus 214, we were speaking about uncommon destinations around the world we would like to visit and we found out one of us was starting the sentence and the other one was completing it, saying exactly what the other person would have said. Although he was not out, he held my hand strongly. I knew it was a big step for him, and also knew he would need a lot more time to get relaxed and used to doing such things. But he was excited too, he had found the courage to do it, because what we were living meant a lot to him.

He was serious and gave me all of his attention. He was pushing me in doing my plans and willing to help me in achieving my goals. I felt these goals were his too, now. He was masculine, into photography and sports, dedicated to working, no gay friends at all.

He loved my paintings, he saw his feelings, his story, his London life reflected into them. We shared dinners with my friend Matthias too.

I never cared much about fashion, so I suppose I was a bit unclassy, wearing tracksuits or cheap clothing. When we were at his place, after breakfast, he loved to put some of the British style clothes he had in his closet on me. We were the same size, even the shoes, and although it started as a joke, I slowly transformed into a good looking gentleman.

We were passing five days a week together, doing a myriad of things. There was some sex, but it was not so frequent. Sex was definitely not driving our relationship. It was sharing the most simple things that gave us precious moments we'll never forget and made us happy.

Sex, which happened once a week, was slow and of high quality, which I was not used to. Before meeting Diego, I had n't had any sexual contact for months. I was just watching porn on my mobile phone before sleeping and I got used to jerking off in about two minutes after the video started. I was trying to cum as fast as possible, and sleep. When I finally found Diego, who was willing to take it slowly, my body was not under my control. As much as I tried to slow it down, my ejaculation was premature and I was always cumming before him. He knew the reason, and he promised me it will get better with time when, when we both manage to relax properly.

He really cared about me, listened to me and got to know me deeper than anyone else, all of that in a relatively short time. We could have been walking through the city for hours, then lying in bed for another many hours, watching some reality show, eating these chips with Modena vinegar we both loved and giving each other a good massage with the cheap coconut oil we had bought at Holland & Barrett before. We cooked together and tried to get used to each other. We have both been single for years and got used to a very individual lifestyle. The first time we slept together it was uncomfortable, almost painful, I was sweating a lot although I usually don't sweat, and he was moving all night searching for a good position, and woke up with pain in the bones. All of this because we hadn't slept together with someone else for a very long time. I loved the warmth of his body, the long hugs, seeing his happy face when waking up. And our life plans made it even more special and meaningful.

He considered his life as his own way of looking for Ithaca, where the destination is only the end of everything, and what is really important is the journey. He truly wanted me to join this journey and share it with him.

And his intentions were really serious.

When I realized that, a voice in my mind started to tell me this was too good to be true.

After all, all my life I didn't deserve to be happy.

Did he lie to me, like everyone else did?

I started to investigate what could be wrong with this story.

I actually started to search deeply, I wanted something to be wrong.

The first thing I didn't like about him was his political orientation. He was conservative, and everyone knows that conservative people judge everyone, at the same time they hide they're doing something much worse.

This is the first reason why I attacked him. He couldn't believe he was being attacked because of his political choices.

With a lot of empathy, he was willing to help me stop smoking. He knew it was a complicated process, and never pointed out how much I smelled, and he was just doing his best in showing me I could live better without that poison. When I met Diego, I won the lottery and now wanted to destroy the prize and throw it away. Since I couldn't believe two gay men could live really happily together in London, where gay life is about individualism, business, career growth, and sex, I started to search for small details and incongruences in what he was saying and doing.

First of all, I've found his CouchSurfing profile. There was one photo of his legs there, and in one photo from the beach, you could see a nipple. I went crazy. From my personal experience on CouchSurfing, many people were using that app to fuck, so I accused him of doing the same. He was shocked, but I finally forced him to delete his profile. And this was just the beginning.

One morning at his place, while I was having breakfast, he went into the shower. When he came out of the bathroom, he was wearing a pair of jocks and a bow tie. He was looking sexy, and he told me he had bought this some years ago on Alibaba, but never wore it. My fucked up brain told me this was not possible. If he had had these jocks at home for years, I was sure he was using them for sexy plays with other people too. When he entered the shower my eyes were full of life, when I saw him coming out, they became shaded. But at that time I still managed to control myself and to come back to reason.

When we met, he was still having Grindr, although he was not using it for hookups. He was actually not opening it at all. When our relationship started to get serious, one evening he deleted the profile in front of me. Months later I created a fake profile, and with a fake GPS app, I was looking for him during his work hours at his workplace. Since I've never found him, I created another profile with a photo of him, waiting to be contacted by some of his ex-lovers. After a few days, I got contacted by someone saying he was my Mexican slut, and that we should meet again. Diego actually had told me that in the last year he only met a Mexican boy, and they didn't have complete sex. Since I really didn't like the expression "Mexican slut", I did a third fake profile on Grindr, contacting the Mexican slut, sending him a photo of a bloke I stole from Instagram and proposing him a bareback fuck. He agreed. I was staying with someone that stayed with someone that used to fuck raw.

I've sent the screenshot of that conversation to Diego, feeling proud I've finally found some proof of what I was accusing him of. He was shocked, but still willing to demonstrate that he was serious in his plans and was monogamous.

But every time he was having lunch with his boss, I was imagining him fucking with some Mexican slut around Baker Street. When he was going to the gym, I was having real panic attacks, loss of breath, imagining him jerking off with some random gym buddy in the steam room. This happens frequently, and everyone who goes to the gym when there are gays knows this.

The biggest panic attack happened by night, during a nightmare. I told him I'll be out of town for his birthday, but I've managed to organize to come back to London before, just in time to arrive at his place at midnight to make him a surprise. But, the night I bought that train ticket I dreamt about my arrival at his house. I knocked on the door and he opened it, naked, with some bloke sleeping in his bed.. This never happened, but my body temperature was over 39 degrees when I woke up.

And every time I was having a panic attack for reasons like that, I was attacking Diego.

The attacks were personal, straight to the most hurting point, the one that was making Diego weak, feeling like shit, slowly lowering his self-esteem. My body would be as hot as hell, me shouting like crazy, not listening to any argument from the other side. I was feeling proud I've discovered he was unfaithful and, although this was not true, I wanted him to feel as bad as I felt. Each of these attacks was completely annihilating my energy. My heartbeat was getting faster, the body temperature rising. I was a monster full of energy during the attack, but my body and mind were exhausted and powerless for days later.

My behavior was too much for him. He loved me, and gave me a lot of opportunities, but my past was stronger. He has let me into his life, given me all his energy to build trust, but I was making him a sad and worried person instead of enjoying what could be shared together.

"If you love me, let me go forever", he told me, begging not to appear anytime again, so he could forget me easier. He also asked me to delete all our photos together, so I'll not fall into the temptation of contacting him again, and to delete his phone number from my contact, so even if I fall into the temptation, I'll not have a way to do it.

I told him if I couldn't stay with him, that meant nobody would ever love me, so I'll start to rent my body for fifty bucks or go to a chemsex orgy. At the time I'd never do either of the two. A few times I thought getting paid for sex would give myself a value, the one nobody was giving me, but I knew this should have been a disgusting experience, and so I never did it.

My last words hurt him so much. But I didn't tell him I was going to fuck for money or bareback on drugs with a lot of strangers to hurt him. It was my way, a completely wrong, to ask him for help, to admit we were born one for each other, and without him, my life would have no sense.

He sent me one last message, wishing that one day he'll pay the entrance to some museum in Hong Kong or New York, and will see my paintings there, but all he wanted now was to forget me.

Although he asked me to throw away all our memories, I still have two souvenirs from him. One is a t-shirt with a Coca-Cola logo he washed after I forgot it at his home. It is still smelling to his detergent, I never wore it or washed it again. The other one is a box of Paracetamol he bought me one day at Tesco when I was having a headache.

Life gave me a person that was willing to get to know me deeply, being on my side, making our dreams happen and being together in fighting our scares. But the small boy from the countryside, in his fucked up brain, couldn't accept that all of this was true. My previous experiences marked me so much that I couldn't trust anyone, and came to the belief that I don't deserve what I always wanted from when I was a child: being happy.

It was hard for me, maybe even impossible, to let myself be loved.

13. CONSERVATIVE ENVIRONMENT

My small town in Poland was a normal place. A person with another color of the skin would be seen once a year, and the locals would be speaking about this for weeks.

As with black or Asian people, there were no faggots. There were only normal people living our normal lives. And everyone knew that, differently from us normal people, faggots were sick. I've heard that a lot of times. In fact, they were doing something totally unnatural.

They were disgusting people, and they were also physically looking disgusting. What I knew was that you needed to take precautions from faggots, because they all wanted to fuck us normal people in the ass. That's what I've been taught, and I was scared of them.

I was not actually sure that faggots really existed because I never met one of them in my life. I was sure of that. If I had met one, I'd know that, I'd have recognized a faggot. Luckily, they were probably living only in big western cities, not here.

When you wanted to insult someone, you'd call him a faggot. In my language, telling someone he's gay is the worst derogatory adjective and the easiest way to show disregard.

The first time I connected this wrong sexual orientation to a name was at school, when the art teacher, speaking about Leonardo Da Vinci, told us some researchers state that he may have been gay. I'll not forget her face while saying this: my teacher was definitely sorry for the poor Leonardo. She was not sorry for him because he may have faced some kind of homophobia, and she was sorry for him being gay. Imagine, he was a very good artist, but he also had the bad luck to be gay.

Again at school, we were analyzing the poetry of an Italian poet, Giovanni Pascoli. After reading his verses *"Saint Lawrence, I know why so many stars in the peaceful air catch fire and fall out, why such great weeping lights in the sky"*, the teacher told us some details about his life. He had a deviant personality, she said. Since nobody in the class understood what deviant personality meant, she explained tu us that he was attracted by other men.

The first time I heard speaking about gays on television was during the funeral of Gianni Versace after he was brutally murdered by his lover. So gays were this, people living a dangerous way of life, always on the edge. And also killing each other.

Other people I knew were gay were Andy Warhol and Elton John, two eccentric artists. And I knew all gays were eccentric. Then there's Freddy Mercury, promoting sinful behavior through his songs, who died of AIDS. All the gays were sinners, sexual maniacs and they were dying of AIDS.

There was no gay in my environment. Gays only were artists, poets, fashion designers living a dark life and being punished. They were all fucking rich and living in big western cities. I was lucky. I was not rich, nobody around me was, so there would be no risk for me.

One light point was a movie I saw at the end of the Nineties about the American Olympic champion Greg Louganis. It was aired on our national TV, although our media has always been the most conservative means of propaganda. It was the first time I ever saw two people from the same sex that can be in a relationship. And the relationship was looking like a heterosexual one, I mean a normal, one. But Greg Louganis died of AIDS, so this was his punishment for belonging to that dark deviant world.

Like other parts of the world where gays are not having an easy life, Poland is a very religious and conservative country. And everyone knows that gays are sinners. As well as perverts. And the Bible says they don't go to Heaven.

Today I'd say church leaders and clergy are using holy scriptures selectively interpreting them as they want, in order to keep the masses motionless. But when I was a child, telling me I'll not go to paradise was one of the biggest psychological threats.

The average citizen of my town in the province was uneducated and uncultured, two of the most loved properties by any politician since that kind of mass of ignorants is the easiest to control.

It is true, from 2011 we have a transgender member in the parliament, Anna Grodzka, and in 2018 there have been twelve gay pride marches around the country. But in some editions, there have been more police members than participants, and in many of them, there have been hundreds of individuals trying to disrupt the celebration by throwing eggs, bottles, bricks and stones at the attendees. In 2004 and 2005 the equality parade was banned. The reasons? The likelihood of counter-demonstrations, interference with religious or national holidays, lacks a permit, among others. Whilst in London being gay is normal, Polish gays they still need to show that they exist.

I remember a time where the few gay bars of the capital were having a secret location, changing every few months. You could get there only if you knew someone that knew where the location was. In these underground places people could really be themselves for a few hours, but always with the fear that some skinheads could discover the place and wait for them at the exit.

I try to imagine myself again walking through the beach and finding out that I'm looking at these male speedos instead of female breasts.

What was going on in my head that day?

It was a total shock. No one of the information I had about gay people was in any way connected to the concept of love.

I was not normal. I was abnormal, actually.

I was a sinner. I was evil. I let the devil possess me.

I'll never not go to paradise. I will go to hell.

I was a pervert.

I was wrong.

I was worthwhile.

I was worthless.

EUSTON, WE HAVE A PROBLEM

I was definitely different. And being different was not a merit, it was something to be ashamed of. A great attack on someone's self-esteem.

I had a problem. And couldn't tell anyone about this.

I was definitely sick.

And that was only the beginning. Many other questions arose. What will the village say if they discover that? People living here are bored, waiting for some new topic to become the trending one. Ruining someone's reputation is a local sport.

Also, could I ever say to my family that I was gay? Nobody knew how they would react. Would they even try to understand it, or would they take me to a doctor? The last one would actually be a good option. I may even get a cure and love girls again, as normal people do.

In a small environment, you're also taught that staying in that place is your destiny. According to locals, big towns are dangerous, and far away, even a place 100 miles away looks as far as the Moon. The environment where you've been born is the only safe place in the world. Only a few people, the strange ones, leave it.

Just a month after I discovered I was gay, I started a part-time job. There was a colleague that, during that autumn, told me the same sentence so many times: "if I was gay, I'd kill myself".

Now this man has a wife and two kids. I haven't seen him in at least a decade. But I'm still waiting to meet him. I want to tell him that I am gay and that, because of that sentence, I could have killed myself fifteen years ago. When you let your ignorance speak, you can hurt a lot. And maybe he is still saying the same sentence to his kids.

With this sentence, I learned I'll need to hide. And for a long while, I could not be myself. And not being yourself means acting. Even if you're the best actor of the world, being on stage every day, on a non-stop performance, is something stressful.

Years ago, I've read some academic research about mental health and LGBT people. There is evidence that shows that, compared with their heterosexual counterparts, gay men and lesbians suffer from more mental health problems, including affective disorders and suicide. The main reason is found in stress as the negative outcome of stigma, marginalization, prejudice, and discrimination.

There are serious scientific studies that show how being a young person who is a sexual minority can still be difficult in a society largely oriented toward heterosexuality, as well as ones explaining how religion may be a source of distress and contribute to internalized homophobia if religious beliefs are irreconcilable with one's sexual identity.

There have also been studies about happiness and life satisfaction in people who identify as gay, lesbian and bisexual in the UK, and they all report much lower levels of well-being than heterosexuals. And we speak about the UK, where being gay is considered normal.

It took me a while to understand that in my town I was not the only gay. I can only wonder how many people were living their lives totally hidden. Each of them has a different life story, but all are driven by pain, provoked by an ignorant society.

I know several people who weren't able to accept themselves. Some of them are now married, with children. I was brave enough to follow my path. But it was not easy.

EUSTON, WE HAVE A PROBLEM

After the first kiss with Pawel and the psycho experience and cum with Olek, I've stayed in my hometown for one more year and I met a few people through that orange chat where photos were not exchanged.

I was looking for a friend, someone to share all I couldn't share with the rest of the world: my thoughts, scares, and doubts. But what I found during that year was only a bunch of cocks to be sucked.

Many of them were saying they were bisexual, not accepting themselves and considering that being gay was something wrong. Having a conversation was almost impossible, it was only meeting, having sex, and leaving. And the precautions people were taking when meeting were so exaggerated to look ridiculous. They would give you an appointment at night, in some big parking lot at a shopping center on the outskirts, which was also the most suspect place to meet someone, instead of a bar or a square in the center of town.

Even if they were not showing a photo, I was lucky. Almost all of the people I met were pretty good looking. We were obviously not fucking in the parking lot. With the car, we were going to remote locations, mostly woods, miles away.

It is funny that in big liberal cities most gays are bottom. In the conservative province, it is the opposite. Almost everyone is top, and there's probably a psychological justification behind it. Something like being top is more masculine and is not so wrong to put your cock inside a hole as could be being fucked.

In most occasions, we fucked without knowing each other's names, then dressed quickly after the act, and left. We were all feeling ashamed after jerking off, like we had done something wrong, something forbidden by common sense and religion, and not accepted by society.

Many of these guys told me that they really enjoyed the time with me and we could repeat it. But, please, if we met somewhere in town, I should not greet them, because nobody needed to know they were gay.

I initially thought they were telling me this because I looked a bit feminine. But that was not the case since I later discovered that most of my masculine gay friends from the deep province lived the same situation. It was just the repression and the fear that anyone could have connected them with the fact of being gay.

Anyway, I felt worthless. And a million times I asked myself why, of eight billion people, I was born as myself, and as gay.

I find it interesting that, although everyone here in London knows that I'm gay without the need to tell them anything, in Poland even today most people would never guess that.

I still feel that the conservative, Catholic, ignorant province of Poland is inside me. I feel like I'm doing something wrong and because of that I don't deserve to be happy, I'm less worthy than my straight friends.

Sometimes I think in the past it was easier. It was not easy to find someone to love, but for that exact reason, when you found someone you matched with, you'd need to make some effort, taking care to maintain that relationship. And people had the possibility to get to know each other deeper.

I'm not saying in the past there were no cheats. But especially in small towns like mine, it was almost impossible to find someone to betray with. If you were able to find one person to share your life and sexuality, you'd take care of it, because it was something to be valued.

Nowadays nobody has any value. We're just fast food meat from the Grindr supermarket. We're cheap material and easy to throw away because something else, much better, is around the corner. And there's no reason to care about the people and their feelings. We can insult them or, easier, block them, not give a shit on how this can affect somebody's self-esteem.

If Poland from the past I'm depicting may seem dark, sometimes I feel London is even darker.

I get sad when I see people in their late sixties and seventies, wearing leather bondage dresses, coming to cruisings in the middle of the night. I don't know what I'll do at their age, but I sincerely hope not to have the need to throw out my cock in a park waiting for it to be sucked. I always hoped to have a partner at that age, but being a realist, I know this may not happen. In that case, I hope I'll play cards with some friends of my age, regardless of the fact that they're gay or straight, sitting at a table in someone's house or in a neighborhood bar. But each of us has its own story. Can I judge these people? Some of them might have lived through at the times of dictators, like Franco in Spain or Ceau☐escu in Romania, when being gay was a crime and being discovered meant was equal to being dead. I suppose that after many years of repressed sexuality, these people feel liberated only now, and they started to live their sexuality in an extreme way at an elderly age, to recover what they have lost when they've been young.

And for younger gays, there seems to be an own standard of normality. A normal gay man goes out to Soho, wears Andrew Christian underwear and ES Collection swimwear, and if you're a really normal gay, your holiday destination will be Mykonos in Greece

All these years in London I felt Matthias, Diego and I were amongst the few gays that were not normal.

I saw myself living in a world of dualities.

When I was in the big city, I missed my family, the children of my sisters, the human warmth the small environment can give you. But then I didn't want to be back to a place where, at Christmas lunch, in my late thirties, people would still be asking me when I'll find a girlfriend to get married too.

The big city was also stressful, too fast, too lonely. I loved walking in nature, connecting with it. It made me feel the absolute peace and feel complete. But then, if I tried to find a good job in a small place, even one that pays half of what my London job is, it was almost impossible. There was not one sushi restaurant in my whole region, neither a good music concert during the whole year.

It's been a long time since I first realized in London I'll never find love. Here everyone looks at themselves, and no matter how good you are, you'll always be a replaceable material. But was it in a small conservative town better? There are only a bunch of gays, and they're ignorant or repressed.

I didn't want to live in a place where I felt so alone, but I also knew I'll never be able to live near my family anymore.

But there was a duality in me that was the worst of all. I was gay and I was a bit homophobic. Conservative Poland was deeply rooted inside me.

EUSTON, WE HAVE A PROBLEM

I was not fitting into that Soho - Mykonos gay world rules, till the moment I didn't start with chemsex. There, for the first time, I felt normal and shared something with people like me. But only now I see it was a total illusion.

14. AFTER THE PARTY

I'm opening my eyes.

There's some light coming out of the curtains. It must be Monday morning already.

My mouth is totally dry. I need water.

I feel pain in each muscle, but I can move. I feel like my head is going to explode.

I move slowly, feeling the heaviness of my body. As I move, the ligaments of my knees are crunching.

The sunlight is not so strong, but it is hurting, like killing my eyes.

I take a glass, bring it to the plug, and fill it with water.

I'm feeling the water slipping through my throat.

That's the moment I realize I am alive.

EUSTON, WE HAVE A PROBLEM

Whatever has happened to me, I am alive.

Only after four more glasses of water my mouth starts to humid again. And I need some sunglasses to protect me from the light.

I'm dying of hunger. I haven't eaten for days. The last thing I ate was on Saturday morning, we shared a pack of chips. I put a couple of eggs to fry and I go back to bed to get my mobile phone.

The light on the phone's screen is hurting a lot. There are four missed calls, three are from the office. There are also two emails, both from my work. One is from yesterday, my boss coldly asked me why I didn't come to work and why I don't pick up the phone. The second one, from today, human resources informing me I got suspended from work.

If the first email is from yesterday, it means today is Tuesday.

I feel like vomiting, my stomach completely empty, looking at the calendar of my phone. Yes, it is Tuesday. I was unconscious for two full days.

Although I'm dying of hunger, my body is so fucked up and I need to force myself to eat these two fried eggs.

I go to the shower.

While the hot water is coming down through my skin, I realize how superficial my life has been during the past half a year. I never had sex sober, even once. And didn't have sex one-to-one for many months.

I have no idea if I passed out, got overdosed or had only fallen asleep, but none of my guests helped me, not even Frank. They just disappeared as rats, to save their fucking assess, careless if I'd survived.

As the water comes down over my body, I see images from my parties. So many times people have been at my place for three days. They have been on PrEP, but although you need to take PrEP daily, many of them never took it during the whole stay at my place. I've never thought about it before.

And I, I was just a sex-addicted, trying to escape from the reality of sadness, but I've fallen into one much worse. All I've done with chems was too easy to reach, happiness would come quickly, and as fast it could disappear. None of these people knew anything about my life or my feelings. Nobody has either noticed my paintings on the wall.

Holding the handle of the shower in my hand, I've realized that I'd stopped doing the things I loved. I couldn't remember the last time I called my mother on Skype. On the easel in my room, there was a painting I started seven months ago, and I've never finished. I also didn't show up for the exam about "Living in the UK". I paid the fifty pound fee to access it, but it was on a Monday, and I was wasted from partying, so I didn't go. I'm sure Diego has already passed that test many months ago.

It was the same with my job. I was there from Monday to Friday, but my mind was totally absent, waiting for the weekend. I lived in a big illusion, convincing myself this was making me feel happy, but it was just the opposite. I lived hundreds of risky situations, and many times I was out of control, I just didn't want to see it. All those shines were fake. The reality is I'm alone.

EUSTON, WE HAVE A PROBLEM

It was all only a big distraction, taking me down the path of perdition through a self-destructive behavior. Before starting all of this, my self-esteem was already below the poverty line.

But it seems this was my way to Ithaca. I needed to pass through all this to get conscious of what I wanted and of how I can achieve it.

Now I see I should have done it differently. Instead of using Grindr, I should have gone to these art expositions, worked on myself on being less shy, and given my attention to people that really show interest in myself as a person.

I go out of the shower and, as I get dry, I feel my muscles are hurting even more. But that makes me happy. I'm alive.

Life has given me a second opportunity, and I was going to use it.

It would take a long time, but I could rebuild my life and return to the roadway. But to do this, I can't go through so much shit alone. I need help. A professional one.

I get dressed and leave my flat.

On my way to the hospital, I take my mobile phone out of my pocket, open WhatsApp and send a message.

"Diego, I know you asked me to disappear, but I miss you a lot".

SOME STATISTICS

London has the most concentrated ChemSex culture in Europe and perhaps globally. Similar trends have been observed in larger cities in Europe, the USA, and Australia.

One in eight gay men in London has HIV and four gay men are being diagnosed in London every day with HIV. One in five people living with HIV doesn't even know they have it.

One gay man in London dies every 12 days as a result of taking drugs associated with chemsex.

Around 3 thousands gay men accessing the Chem Sex Support at 56 Dean Street in London each month are using chemsex drugs, 70 percent of whom are unable or unwilling to have sober sex.

Although nobody dies of AIDS today, in 2017, 940 thousand people died of HIV-related issues. Tuberculosis is the leading cause of death among people living with HIV.

At least one-third of the 37 million people living with HIV worldwide are infected with latent TB. Globally, people living with HIV are 26 times more likely to develop active TB disease than those without HIV.

EUSTON, WE HAVE A PROBLEM

In 2017, 1,8 million people got infected by HIV.

When taken daily, Pre-Exposition Profilaxis (PrEP) totally protects against HIV infection. It is possible to buy it privately online, but now more than 10,000 people get it for free. From the commercialization of PrEP, new HIV cases in developed areas have almost halved.

However, PrEP alone doesn't protect from any other STI and is meant to be used in combination with condoms.

With PrEP, a lot of the concern around HIV transmission has been reduced, which resulted in a rise of condomless sex, orgies and chemsex.

Condomless sex is leading to a rise in syphilis, chlamydia, gonorrhea and hepatitis C.

In March 2018 a report from England's public health agency described a case of gonorrhea that was resistant to both components of the dual antibiotic therapy of azithromycin and ceftriaxone — the only remaining recommended treatment for gonorrhea. In the following months, two similar cases have been reported in Australia.

Anyone who takes illegal drugs is putting their health at risk.

As the substances are unregulated, there is no way to be certain that people are buying them in a safe form.

Not only do users run the risk of becoming addicted, overdosing on drugs can be fatal.

ABOUT THE AUTHOR

ADAM KACZINSKY

Born in a conservative country in 1984, he is left-handed, gay and sometimes a bit homophobic. Although his dream is to become a best-selling author, he's only writing as a therapy, obliged by his psychologist.

If you want to contact the author, you can write to him at the e-mail address adam.kaczinsky@gmail.com.